SURVIVAL OF THE SICKEST

JORDAN VEZINA

Copyright © 2022 by Jordan Vezina

All rights reserved.

No part of this book may be reproduced in any form or by any electronic or mechanical means, including information storage and retrieval systems, without written permission from the author, except for the use of brief quotations in a book review.

Cover by: Deranged Doctor Design

PROLOGUE

SHEILA TIGHTENED her grip on the fixed blade Gerber knife and tried to slow her breathing. She had to keep reminding herself this wasn't the first bad spot she'd been in, either before the virus or since. However, if any of them had been worse than this, she was having a hell of a hard time remembering them.

Across the street, she could see the ring of keys hanging from Wilson's belt. On that ring, mixed in with all the others, was the key that unlocked the armory. She'd always thought it was a bad idea to have every weapon secured in that one room, particularly when the only key—aside from the one Roland had on him—was carried by Wilson. Roland had insisted Wilson was the 'key master,' and that was just the way things were done.

Of course, the sentries outside the walls carried weapons, but Sheila doubted they were faring any better than she was. At the beginning of the attack, there had been a handful of shots fired, but nothing since then. It had all happened too fast.

If she was going to survive this mess, Sheila knew she had to get that key from Wilson, get into the armory, and, as the room's name implied, arm herself. She definitely needed something more substantial than the battle knife she was holding or the axe her compatriot Robert wielded.

Getting the key from Wilson wasn't actually the problem.

The dilemma was how to get past the five black-eyed cannibals who were currently eating him.

"Why the hell are they taking so long?" Robert asked as he knelt beside Sheila in the alleyway. "They ripped through everyone else like a damn buzzsaw. Why don't they just finish their meal and move on?"

"Maybe Wilson's tougher to chew," Sheila replied as she leaned out to look down the street.

The dead were everywhere. To be more specific, *pieces* of the dead were everywhere. Robert wasn't wrong; whatever these things were, they were shredding everyone in their path. According to the last reliable count, there were roughly five hundred souls in the town of Oatmeal, making it one of the largest satellite communities in the United States. Fifty of those souls had opted in for the second generation of Pandemify, which meant they now had fifty of these rabid things killing the other four hundred and fifty residents of the town.

Robert looked down the street and shook his head. "It's *three blocks* to the armory. Even if we do get the keys, there's no way we'll make it through those things."

"There is if we stick to the middle of the street," Sheila clarified. "No point trying to get back to cover. Once we're out there, we're out there. Might as well just run to the end zone. That's what you say, right?"

"Yeah," Robert said with a weak smile. "Straight to the end zone."

Robert had played ball for the Texas A&M Aggies back in the day, before civilization went down the toilet. He stood about six foot tall and was built like a bus, but despite being so big, he was lightning fast. Sheila had seen it for herself. She thought about that for a moment, about how back when she was playing den mother to one of the top motorcycle clubs in Baton Rogue, Louisiana, she wouldn't even have taken the time to set someone like Robert on fire, much less talk to him. Now, they were depending on each other to stay alive.

"Okay," Sheila said. "That's what we're doing, then."

She turned to Robert and looked him in the eyes. His skin was ashen. He felt her stare and snapped out of it.

"I'm scared," he said abruptly.

"It's all right, honey," Sheila said reassuringly. "I'm scared, too, but we have to do it. If we don't, it's only a matter of time before those things find us. Hope ain't a plan. Are you pickin' up what I'm layin' down?"

Robert nodded his head.

"You're my blocker," Sheila said. "I'm gettin' those keys, come hell or high water, and I'm going to assume you'll keep those things off of me."

"You can count on me," Robert said. "No matter what."

Sheila stared at him for a moment and then nodded. She took a deep breath and then let it out. She knew the drill by now; knew what it took to do something as dumb as this.

Don't think about it. Just go.

And that's what she did. She turned from Robert, drove her foot into the ground, and sprinted out into the open. The five black-eyed cannibals were still ahead of her, working on Wilson's body.

Then she saw something that chilled her to the bone.

Wilson's eyes turned toward her.

Jesus! she thought. *He's still alive!*

What happened next was like something out of a movie. If she'd thought about it for even a moment, there's no way Sheila would have done something so foolish, but she wasn't thinking. She leapt into the air and landed hard, driving her knife through the top of the head of the cannibal closest to her.

She felt a *whoosh* beside her and knew without looking it was Robert's axe swinging through the air past her head.

It found its mark.

Despite the fact there were at least three more of these monsters within arm's reach of her, Sheila ignored her survival reflex and went for the keys on Wilson's belt. She felt fingertips brushing her shoulder and knew one of the cannibals had almost gotten a hold of her, but Robert had stepped in to pull him away.

For just a moment, her eyes met Wilson's, a single tear rolling down his left cheek.

"*Kill ... me,*" he gurgled.

It all happened so fast. The keyring came loose from his belt, and Sheila broke from her kneeling position and sprinted forward down the street, toward the armory. She trusted Robert was behind her, still blocking them.

He was.

One of the black-eyed cannibals ran out of a building beside her, and Sheila watched in horror as Robert raced ahead of her and tackled the creature to the ground. There was no time to look back; no time to see how he was doing.

How far had she run? At least a block, maybe more. Her heart was beating out of her chest, and her vision was blurred.

Then she saw them streaming out of the buildings and the side streets around her.

There was no time to think; no time to estimate if she could possibly make it to her destination before they overtook her. There were at least two dozen of them behind her, running like rabid dogs racing after a meal.

There was no way Robert had made it.

Then, just like a sliver of hope emerging from a

nightmare, Sheila saw the door in front of her. Without meaning to, she had pivoted to the left, toward the door to the old City Jail. The building had stood for more than a century, a relic from a time long past, with old iron bars on the window and everything. Sheila burst through the door and, just as quickly, turned and slammed it shut. No sooner had she thrown the deadbolt in place than the entire door rattled on its frame.

The cannibals were throwing themselves against the door, hammering at it with their fists. Already the wooden door was starting to splinter.

Sheila turned and moved down the dimly lit hallway to the old armory at the far end of the building. She rifled though the keys, looking for the oldest one; the key that would unlock the door to her survival.

But what was she going to do once she was inside? There were at least twenty of those things out there. If they all crowded into the building, would she really be able to take them on?

Sheila knew how that would end.

She suddenly wished she hadn't dropped her pistol after she'd run out of rounds when this had first started. That had been dumb. Not that the weapon would have done her any good at this exact moment, but she would have been able to replenish the nine millimeter ammo she needed from the cache in the armory.

Her hands trembled as Sheila worked the key in the lock, the pounding at the other end of the hallway behind her growing increasingly louder. She could hear the door breaking apart. If she were back out on the street, at least she'd have a fighting chance, but in a hallway like this, she would be easily overwhelmed. Within minutes, there would be nothing left of her but bones and a pool of blood.

Click.

At the exact moment the tumbler in the lock fell into place, she heard a crash behind her and a subsequent chorus of growls.

The black-eyed cannibals had breached the door.

With no time to look back, and no time to assess her options, Sheila stepped into the room and grabbed the closest weapon to her, a Mossberg twelve gauge shotgun. She hoped to God it was loaded.

She spun on her heel, brought the firearm up to her shoulder, and pulled the trigger.

The slug ripped through the head of a cannibal barely more than a foot from her.

Sheila stepped back as she racked another round

into the chamber and kicked at the door to slam it shut. She could see several of the things piling into the hallway. If they trapped her inside the armory, it would be the end of her.

An arm reached in the door, and she heard the sickening snap of a bone breaking as the limb stopped the door from closing. Sheila wedged her foot against the door, and without thinking, she slid the barrel through the opening and pulled the trigger.

The concussive blast of the shotgun within the room full of steel was enough to blow her eardrums out, yet Sheila racked and fired the shotgun two more times before the doorway was clear and she was able to slam it shut. It automatically locked in place.

Sheila felt the shotgun fall to the ground with a clatter as she dropped to her knees and put her hands to her ears. The high-pitched ringing was deafening, but it felt almost as if she were hearing the sound underwater. She took her hands away from her ears and saw a mix of blood and clear fluid. Her heartbeat raced as she tumbled to the hard concrete.

Sheila looked up at the ceiling and could feel herself slipping into unconsciousness. Yet, even as her vision began to ebb, she heard a voice in her head, speaking softly.

It was a woman's voice.

Somehow, Sheila knew it wasn't just a hallucination. It was real. The voice was as real as any she had ever heard.

"*Come to me,*" the woman said. "*Walk into the sun. Find me in the woods.*"

Harris Hawthorne and Bob sat in the tree line beyond the rear gate that led into Cypress Mill, roughly twenty meters away from the open field that bridged the two. They had been there for over an hour, with the rest of the boys another fifty meters behind them. They had taken the long way around and then hiked two miles through the woods so they wouldn't be seen by either the casual observer or the trained eye.

Harris had to admit he was pretty pleased with himself and how they had pulled this off. Granted, their number was a little lighter than they had been in the beginning—at this point, down to about twenty, total—but those numbers would soon be replenished. They just had to bluff the appearance of having a much larger force and convince whoever remained in Cypress Mill to surrender. It was classic guerrilla warfare.

Granted, the boys were all running on no sleep, they were hungry, and they were tired from what little fighting they had done against the Nephilim before skinning out of Dodge. Still, they were excited, and that was more than enough to keep the charge in their batteries.

Bob looked through his binoculars at the town, put them down, and then shook his head.

"What is it?" Harris asked.

"Same thing as back at the house," Bob replied. "Too quiet."

"It's still early," Harris remarked. "Maybe they just ain't up and about yet."

"Maybe," Bob agreed. "Or maybe something else is going on."

"It's possible Randall Eisler called them out as reinforcements and we just didn't cross paths with them on our way in. They're mostly fighters. They don't have a big community like Oatmeal does."

"True," Bob replied and nodded his head. "Still."

Harris picked up the binos and had a look for himself. He had to admit, it *was* strange. There was nothing; no sign of movement. He checked his watch again. It was almost nine in the morning. That didn't quite jibe with his theory about the residents of Cypress Mill still being in bed, but perhaps he had been right about them all going out on the warpath.

"Either way," Harris said, "don't matter much. Can't turn back now."

"You can always turn back," Bob said. "No one will question that."

Harris looked at his second-in-command for a moment and then shook his head.

"No, can't turn back now," Harris reaffirmed. "I don't disagree with you, and I know the boys will understand, but all the same, what if we could just roll in there and take it? What if there was no resistance, and it was ours for the taking? What if all that was true and we didn't do it?"

"What if it's a trap?" Bob countered.

"Then it's a trap we're about to walk into. But *I'll* be the one to stick my head into the lion's mouth first."

"What do you mean by that?" Bob asked.

Harris unslung his rifle and handed it to Bob.

"What the hell are you playing at?" Bob demanded.

"Building a future," Harris responded. He pulled a walkie-talkie from his pocket and keyed it once. The walkie clipped to Bob's vest crackled.

"You can't be serious?" Bob said.

"We'll find out real quick," Harris said as he stood up. "If I get shot in the head, probably best not to join me."

The rear gate into Cypress Mill wasn't quite as structured as the front entrance, with its jack-knifed big rig. The rear entrance was just a simple cattle gate that had been set up across the single lane road that led into town. Granted, there was concertina wire strung all around it and what looked like a makeshift guardhouse, but it was unlikely to keep a determined party out.

Harris stopped a dozen feet from the guardhouse. He looked over his shoulder to where he had come from the tree line. More and more, he was starting to think Bob was right. It was too damn quiet in this town. Even if they had sent reinforcements to the farmhouse, there would still be *some* people left. Wouldn't there?

He turned back to the gate and walked up to it. The lock was still secured, but getting over a cattle gate wasn't exactly a herculean feat. Seeing as it was the only thing on this stretch of road not covered in razor wire or with some other obstacle in the way,

Harris clambered his way over it and landed on the other side without ceremony.

For some reason, he'd thought something would happen the moment he actually set foot on the ground inside of Cypress Mill. He wasn't exactly expecting a welcoming party ... but *something*.

Instead, there was nothing. Just dead silence.

Damien felt like they had been waiting on Bob and Harris to make a move for hours.

Now that Harris was finally doing something, at least they'd be moving soon. Maybe that would also mean getting a full meal. The problem with the whole cannibal gig was that they couldn't exactly carry beef jerky in their pockets to snack on. Granted, some of the boys had mentioned doing something like that a while back, but it had seemed a little unwarranted seeing as there were was no shortage of dead bodies scattered throughout the Texas Meat Belt.

It's damn quiet in these woods, Damien thought. Why the hell was it so quiet? He reached out and tapped Vince Welch on the shoulder.

"What is it?" Vince asked.

"Shouldn't there be animals?"

"What the hell are you talking about?"

"In the woods," Damien went on. "Shouldn't there be animals?"

"Is this some kind of damn riddle?" Vince asked, clearly annoyed.

"Listen." Damien gestured all around them. "I don't hear nothin'."

"We've got bigger things to worry about," Vince scoffed. "Get your head in the game."

"Right," Damien said and nodded. "Look, I'm gonna take a leak."

"Just keep your ears open," Vince said. "We'll be steppin' off any minute now."

Harris had been standing at the gate for at least a full three minutes before he finally stepped forward. He tapped the pistol secured to his right hip in its Kydex holster. He was starting to think that leaving his AR behind had been a bad idea. It had made sense when he'd handed it to Bob in the woods, but it sure felt like a lot had changed since then.

The main road into Cypress Mill stretched out about a hundred more feet in front of him before it hit the first two buildings. One was a big old brick structure that looked like it had been some kind of a warehouse, and the other was a big metal building that Harris knew was their 'Processing House.' It was the place they took anyone their hunting parties came across, to decide who would join the community and who would become food. Harris knew that most of the time, it was the latter.

Harris turned back and couldn't see Bob or any of his men at the tree line. That was good. It meant they were observing the rules of cover and concealment. He turned back to the road and waited a moment. Still nothing. Not a single noise.

"Sack up," Harris said to himself quietly and walked forward.

He moved carefully along the old road, making sure to stay away from the middle of it and keep his head on a swivel. The last thing he needed was to be ambushed. Within a few minutes, he could smell the Processing House. It was just like he remembered. Without question, they were stacking the dead in there.

Harris stopped close to the main door and thought about drawing his pistol, but then decided against it. The whole point of leaving the AR behind was to attempt some diplomacy, so that he could recruit whoever was still around to his team. Plus, all he had to do was let out a yell, and he'd have the boys at his back within a matter of minutes.

The door to the Processing House was partially closed, but a flow of fresh blood ran from inside, out into the dirt, where it had pooled into a thick brown mud. Harris reached forward with his left hand, careful to keep his right hand beside his pistol. He pulled the door open with a creak of the rusted hinges and then froze.

"*Jesus,*" he whispered.

A headless body lay on the concrete, but it wasn't some random person who'd been scooped up by a hunting party. This was Kevin, the head of the Slaughterhouse Five. Harris recognized him by his leather apron. He'd met the man when Randall Eisler had given him a tour of the community. He'd seemed like kind of a head case, a little too into his work, even for Harris.

"Have you ever killed an animal?"

Harris's head snapped up toward the voice coming from the semi-darkness. His hand went for his pistol.

"You'll be dead before you hit the floor," June Kennedy hissed.

She was now face-to-face with him. How had she moved so fast? She stared blankly at Harris with her coal black eyes. She was covered in blood, her soaked dress sticking to her flesh. She reached out slowly, took the pistol from its holster, and tossed it away.

"You can feel it, can't you?" she asked.

"Feel what?" Harris asked.

June walked past him and out into the street. "That you're no match for me," she continued. "That there's no point in fighting."

Harris looked into the Processing House and could see bodies everywhere, each one missing its head. He turned back to June. Steam was rising from her body. What the hell had happened to this woman?

She stood in the street, looking out toward the tree line Harris had approached from.

"You can watch if you want," June teased. "But, to be honest, if I were you, I'd probably look away."

Harris frowned, her cryptic words making little sense. "What are you talking about?"

Then he heard the first shot ring out, followed by another, and another, and another. He looked to the tree line and saw his men breaking from it, running into the field, seemingly with no direction or organization. A moment later, he understood why.

They were being chased.

There were dozens of people pursuing them,

but there was something wrong with the way they moved. The trailing figures were running with jerky, almost animal-like movements. Some of the boys were firing at them, but seemingly with no effect.

Then the first of the boys was taken down. Three of the pursuers were on top of him, battering him with their fists, almost like gorillas. Harris could see the man's body starting to come apart.

"*Jesus*," he cursed quietly.

"He can't hear you. Not in this place."

Harris looked to his pistol laying on the ground and then back to the field. Somehow he knew June was right. He'd be dead before he even touched it. The realization sent a cold shock of fear racing up his spine.

More of the boys were being taken down. Ahead of them, he could see Bob in a dead sprint. He had dropped his rifle to be faster. The man looked as if he might make it, but to where, Harris had no idea. Then one of the creatures gained on him, reached forward, and swiped at his head.

It came clean off.

Harris felt his breath catch in his throat. All of the boys were dead, and this pack was now eating them where they fell in the field—but not like Harris and the rest of the boys always had. This was ... *wild*, for lack of a better word.

He felt a hand on his shoulder, making him jump.

"Have you ever?" June asked. "Killed an animal?"

"I ... I don't want to die," Harris managed.

"You won't," June replied with a smile. "At least, not right away."

Harris turned back to the field and saw the pack of black-eyed cannibals moving forward again.

Moving toward him.

"You can run if you like," June said, stepping back from Harris. "Outcome will be the same."

Despite this admonition, Harris turned and broke into a run down Main Street. The street was L-shaped and turned a hard left that would take him into the heart of the town. Harris made the turn, and as he ran, he felt the ground tremor beneath him. He didn't have to look back. He knew what it was.

Dozens of the black-eyed cannibals were thundering toward him.

Ahead, the dead were everywhere. Harris slowed down, his brain taking a moment to process what he was seeing. It wasn't just dead bodies he was looking at; it was *pieces* of bodies. Arms, legs, torsos, and other things that were unrecognizable but had at one point clearly been part of a person. The streets were stained red, to the point where it looked like a red carpet had been rolled out for Satan himself.

Somewhere deep inside of him, Harris could feel his survival instincts kicking in. There was no more conscious thought; only reflex. To his right, the door to a building was cracked open. Harris pivoted hard and pushed his way through it, then turned, slammed it, and locked it.

He knew he couldn't outrun them. The demons were too damn fast. He thought back to all the zombie movies he had loved as a kid. They were always so slow on the big screen. Not like this.

Harris turned again and ran through the building, already hearing the sounds of fists hammering on the door behind him. A few dozen steps took him out the back door and onto an adjoining street. He turned again and ran away from the building.

This street was no different from the previous. Bodies were scattered, appearing as though they had tried to mount some sort of resistance here, but it had obviously failed. Harris slowed down just enough to snatch a rifle and a few magazines from a torso he found before continuing his sprint. He knew where he was going; it was just a matter of whether or not he could get there.

Harris could feel he was already soaked in sweat. On top of that, he could feel the beginnings of hunger pangs. How long had it been since he'd eaten? He should have eaten before they'd tried going after Cotton in that house, but he'd been in such a damn hurry. Now, he was paying for it.

Running down the street, Harris looked ahead of him and could see his reflection in a parked car. More importantly, he could see what was behind him. The cannibals had caught up with him. He probably only had a hundred meters of stand-off distance.

Finally, ahead of him, he saw what he was looking for: the jack-knifed big rig that blocked the main road into Cypress Mill. It was splattered with blood, and he could see a dead man atop the tractor trailer. Somehow, the creatures had even gotten to him up there.

That was fine, because that wasn't where Harris was headed.

He briefly wondered if he should try to lay down some suppressive fire, maybe buy himself an extra minute or two, but he quickly decided against it. No, something was different about these black-eyed cannibals. They weren't afraid. Harris got the distinct impression that even if he fired on them and was getting hits, it wouldn't slow them down.

Harris ran around the front of the big rig that was laying on its side and scrambled up to the driver's side door. He turned and grabbed at the handle. He could see the waves of black-eyed cannibals racing toward him, and he hoped to hell the door wasn't locked.

It wasn't. He felt the *click* of the handle as he depressed the button, and with no little effort, he pulled the heavy door up far enough for him to squeeze inside. He slid the AR in first and then lowered himself into the cabin, closing the door behind him.

No sooner had he locked the door than he felt a heavy thump against the vehicle as the first cannibals slammed into the windshield. Even though he knew they couldn't break it, he still reflexively jumped back and flattened himself against the back of the cab.

Harris knew they couldn't break the window because it was bulletproof. All of the windows in the truck were. He remembered this from the tour Randall Eisler had given him the first time the man proposed Harris and the boys join him at Cypress Mill.

Back when things first started falling apart, the government had issued grants to long-haul truck drivers to reinforce their vehicles, to keep the drivers —and more importantly, the goods they transported —as safe as possible. When society had unraveled, it hadn't taken long for highwaymen to become a problem and for cartels to start hitting trucks close to the Southern border. The government had understood that if the trucks stopped running, things would deteriorate at an inconceivable pace. The federal grants had financed the installation of bulletproof glass and armor panels. Most drivers even started having security guards ride shotgun with them. Some men liked the company on the long drives, but even those that didn't understood the utility.

Harris watched the screaming horde of black-eyed cannibals pounding on the windshield. They didn't seem to be getting tired like he'd hoped they would. He glanced around the cabin, surveying his options, but Harris knew it was hopeless. He wasn't sure how long he would be able to hold out like this.

Then it stopped. Harris stared at the horde through the windshield. The cannibals were all just standing there, as if waiting for something. Another minute passed and then they all stepped to the side, reminiscent of the parting of the Red Sea.

June Kennedy walked between the parted waves of black-eyed cannibals, her eyes locked on Harris. She walked to the windshield and placed her hand against it, then pulled it back, leaving a bloody handprint in its wake.

She looked around the cabin and then back to Harris.

"How long do you think you can hold out?" June asked.

"In here?" Harris replied. "Long as I need to."

"Not in there," June said. "Out here."

"Looks like we won't find out," Harris said confidently. "Because I feel downright at home in here, and I ain't coming out."

June stepped back from the truck and smiled.

"You have to come out someday," she said. "And your day is over. Your kind are on borrowed time. Do you know what every empire in history has in common?"

"Ask me if I give a shit!" Harris snapped.

June's smile faded. "It died."

CHAPTER 1

Cotton Wiley had decided to let April take the wheel for the trip out to Cypress Mill from the farmhouse. It wasn't just because he was tired, or that he hadn't driven a car in months; something else was going on, and it was hard to describe. He'd felt off-balance for years. The feeling came and went, but it never really amounted to anything serious. This was different, though. It was almost as if the environment was shifting around him and his brain couldn't keep up with it.

If he was being honest with himself, Cotton had never really taken all of the other brain issues he'd had before seriously. He either tried to push past them, wait them out, or do a little self-medicating.

Now, he could feel those strategies would no longer be options.

His mind flashed back to the breathing exercises he'd been taught at NICoE—The National Intrepid Center of Excellence—at the Bethesda Naval Hospital. Around the time he was wrapping up his service, most of the guys who fit Cotton's operational profile were being put through there. He knew it was a great program and had helped a lot of men like him, but even while he was going through it, he didn't think he needed to be there. He was Cotton damn Wiley, not some PTSD head case who needed to do art therapy and yoga to keep him from putting a gun in his mouth.

Now, though, he was beginning to think he had been wrong about that.

Cotton looked over his shoulder through the rear windshield and saw Jean sitting in the back of the SUV, the rear hatch open and her eyes scanning the horizon. She was on her game, more so now than ever before. He was also realizing just how much she knew about weapons and tactics. At twelve years old, Jean had more close combat experience than some

SEALs he'd worked with, especially prior to the Global War on Terror.

Their vehicle was in the middle of the caravan, and Cotton knew Roland had set it up that way to offer them the greatest degree of protection in case they were hit. So far, everything seemed kosher with his old Command Master Chief, and Cotton could feel himself trusting the man again.

Jorge and the kid, Brian, had split from the group to head out for Tow. Cotton remembered what April had said about wanting to join the community of Gatherers there and had wondered if she would try to go with them once Roland announced where the two men were heading. Instead, she hadn't even batted an eye. She seemed committed to staying with Cotton and June for the duration.

Cotton knew that Randall Eisler had been trying to contact his people in Cypress Mill via the radio and was still having no luck. It was probably nothing—atmospherics could play havoc with even the best comms system—and the sets they were using were nowhere near the best. Still, Cotton kept his guard up. Who knew what they were about to drive into? They were also assuming they had wiped out the Nephilim at the farmhouse, but if they hadn't, it wouldn't be a stretch to believe that it could have been just the beginning of a bigger attack.

"*All vehicles, stop!*" a voice crackled from the radio in the truck, as well as the one Cotton had stowed in his chest rig.

April applied pressure to the brake, and the vehicle slowed in sync with the rest of the trucks in the caravan.

"What's happening?" Jean asked, but she kept her eyes on her sector. She knew not to abandon her observation post.

"Not sure," Cotton replied as he picked up the radio from the dash. "SITREP."

Cotton had called for a situation report. He didn't expect a perfect recitation according to SEAL doctrine, but he knew it would get the message across to Roland Reese and Randall Eisler.

There was quiet for a moment. Cotton leaned forward but couldn't see much past the vehicles in front of them.

"*Someone in the road*," Roland's voice came back on the radio. "*Not a marauder. Cotton, meet me at the front.*"

"Roger that," Cotton replied and set the radio back in its cradle.

"Should I come?" Jean asked.

"No," Cotton said as he opened his door and stepped out into the road. "Stay here. We don't know what this might turn into. If it goes south, be ready to make it hot."

He took a moment to adjust his gear, tightening the back strap on the Haley chest rig and adjusting the sling that held his DDM4 to him. He walked forward, down the line of vehicles, and found Roland standing in the road with Randall Eisler. Another two hundred yards along, he saw a man standing behind a single barricade. It wasn't even much of a barricade at that. It was just a simple wooden sandwich board.

Cotton stopped and scanned the area around him.

"Already on it," Roland said. "Can't see anyone out there."

"But we know there is," Randall Eisler countered. "No one's crazy enough to pull a stunt like this without backup."

"FPAR?" Cotton asked, indicating the Free People of the American Republic.

"Don't know who the hell they're fighting at this point," Randall Eisler scoffed. "Federal government is basically destroyed."

"It's the cities now," Roland said. "They want a do-over."

"A do-over?" Cotton asked.

"Kind of the same thing I wanted," Roland said with a shrug. "But they really want to wipe the slate. Total destruction of any functioning government, and then see what rises from the ashes."

"That's fucking stupid." Randall Eisler laughed. "I'll tell you *exactly* what it'll be. The Russians and the Chinese duking it out in Kansas."

"Why Kansas?" Cotton asked with a raised eyebrow.

"Geographical center of the United States," Randall Eisler answered.

"That makes no sense."

"You're standing in the middle of Texas arguing with a cannibal about the Russians and Chinese having a showdown in the middle of the United States," Randall Eisler continued. "I think *anything* making sense at this point is out the window."

"Fair enough," Cotton agreed with a nod.

"If it is FPAR," Roland said, pretending as if the preceding conversation had never happened, "they're anti-vaxxers, which means non-cannibals."

"Which means I'm the designated spokesperson," Cotton concluded.

"I knew there was a reason I made you a team leader back in the day," Roland said with a smile.

"And then fired me."

"Five times," Roland said, holding up four fingers and a thumb. "If I'm not mistaken."

"What am I supposed to say to him?"

"The truth," Roland said. "We're just a mix of normals and mild-mannered cannibals on our way back to our community. No government affiliation, and no threat to them."

"And if things go sideways?" Cotton asked.

Roland became serious. "You know I've got you covered,"

"And who's got you covered?"

"You know," Roland said, "I've been wondering that myself lately."

Cotton walked back to the truck and leaned in the passenger side window.

"Possible FPAR in the road. Roland and Eisler want me to be the ambassador and get us through."

April looked around the landscape. "Just the one?"

"Nah," Cotton said. "It's never just one. The rest are probably laid up in an ambush position, waiting to see which way the wind blows." He looked back to where Jean was positioned in the back seat. "You're on me."

His daughter was surprised. "Really?"

"Right now, you're the only person here I actually trust with my life." He turned back to April. "No offense."

"None taken," April replied, though that wasn't the entire truth.

Jean clambered out of the side door with her MK18 and a small Jansport backpack she had reconfigured into a makeshift assault pack. It contained a handful of magazines—AR and pistol—in the outer pouch and a bottle of water, an MRE, and her gas mask stashed in the larger compartment. They hadn't needed the latter yet, but Jean increasingly believed in being prepared for every eventuality.

Cotton turned from the truck and walked back to the front of the line with his daughter beside him.

"I'm gonna walk up on him," Cotton said. "I want you to lag about thirty yards behind. If anything goes wrong, you hit the ground and lay down suppressive fire. Don't worry about my position; just make it rain."

"'Make it rain?'" Jean asked with a raised eyebrow. "What does that mean? Like ... rain bullets?"

Cotton stopped and looked down at her. "Yeah. That's what it means."

He made a mental note not to use strip club references with his young daughter. Clearly, some of the habits he had developed working with his fellow SEALs for all those years were particularly hard to break.

Jorge slowed his truck at the entrance to the Highway 29 bridge that would take them into the town of Tow. He knew that the community had been established on a small peninsula on the Colorado river, and that the bridge was generally manned by a couple of 'greeters.'

Sure enough, as he brought the truck to a stop, he a man who looked to be in his mid-sixties wearing overalls and sitting on a stool on the right lane of the bridge. He was reading a book and seemed completely unaware of their arrival.

Brian leaned forward in his seat. "What the hell is he doing?"

"He's the town greeter," Jorge replied.

"The what?"

"Town greeter," Jorge repeated. "They do things a little differently out here."

"Where's his gun?" Brian asked.

"These people don't believe in guns."

"Don't *believe* in them? They're firearms, not fucking leprechauns!"

Jorge couldn't help but laugh. The kid was starting to grow on him.

"Look, I get that it's weird, but somehow they've gotten by so far. The people here do some stuff for Roland to keep on his good side, so we're checking in."

Jorge stepped out of the truck and waited for the Greeter to take notice of him. When the older man didn't, Jorge slammed the door to the truck.

The Greeter looked up from his book and smiled. "Welcome, friend!" he called out.

"You've gotta be shitting me," Brian said, under his breath.

"Cool it," Jorge said. "We've just gotta have a look around, check this chore off our list, and then get on the road to Oatmeal."

"Why do I think it won't be that easy?" Brian asked.

The Greeter walked toward the two strangers

and extended his hand. "I'm Reginald," the man offered.

Jorge and Brian both shook Reginald's hand in turn.

"I'm Jorge," he said affably. "And this is Brian."

Reginald looked the two men up and down. They both appeared as if they had been through a war—mainly because they had.

"You look a little worse for wear," Reginald observed. "The two of you do."

"We ran into a little trouble down the road," Jorge said. "Nothing we couldn't handle."

Reginald's eyes were drawn to the Colt 1911 pistol on Jorge's hip.

"I can see that." He looked around and then back to Jorge. "Something I can help you with?"

"If I recall correctly, your leader's name is Mike Whitcomb?" Jorge asked.

"We don't really have leaders and followers here," Reginald corrected. "We believe in a more holistic society."

Jorge shot Brian a look to silence him.

"I didn't say anything," Brian blurted.

"You were going to," Jorge said and then turned back to Reginald. "Regardless, I need a word with him."

Reginald's eyes returned to the pistol. "It's just ... We don't carry guns here," he said slowly. "I'd need you to leave that behind." He nodded toward Jorge's Colt.

"Can't quite say I'm comfortable with that," Jorge said. "You understand. End of the world and all."

"Regardless," Reginald said, echoing Jorge's words, "town rules."

Jorge sighed. "No way around it?"

"Not that I can see."

Jorge pulled the Colt from its holster with two fingers and handed it to Brian.

"Wait with the truck," Jorge said as Brian took the pistol. "If I'm not back in an hour, you come looking."

"Roger that," Brian replied.

Jorge walked with Reginald across the old stone bridge and down a country road that led into what most considered the formal town of Tow. There were other areas and neighborhoods scattered around the coastline of the Colorado river, but the town itself was little more than a cluster of buildings in this central spot.

It was just as Jorge had expected it would be, perhaps even more so. There wasn't a weapon in sight, and the people seemed to almost be living in the Sixties. The old post office was situated at the end of Main Street, and had been converted into the de facto town hall.

"This is it," Reginald said as they approached the building. He stopped in the street and showed no signs of intending to accompany Jorge inside.

"You're not coming in?" Jorge asked.

Reginald looked up at the sun for a moment and then back to Jorge. "No, it's almost nine. I have a class."

"A class?"

"I teach knitting under the old oak tree at the end of the street."

Jorge smiled. "You're fucking with me."

Reginald looked confused. "What do you mean?"

"Never mind." Jorge sighed and turned back to the town hall.

He pushed the door open and walked inside, to find an older man sitting behind the mail counter. His eyeglasses were pushed up on his forehead as he surveyed an old leather-bound book. Jorge couldn't help but notice a familiar smell, remembering it from way back, during his woodworking days. It was the smell of rich mahogany.

The man at the postal counter looked up at him. His demeanor was noticeably different to Reginald's. This man was clearly not happy to see Jorge.

"Mike Whitcomb, I presume?" Jorge asked.

Mike closed the book and sat back on his stool. "You presume correctly,"

'The King sent me."

Mike studied Jorge for a moment and then nodded. "I understand," Mike said. "I'm guessing he wants to check on his investment."

Jorge remained silent. Mike cocked his head to the side.

"You don't know, do you?" Mike asked.

"Whatever that's about," Jorge replied, "it's not why I'm here. Some shit went down last night out by Round Rock. He just sent me here to make sure things didn't spill over into your community."

"That explains why you're out of sorts," Mike observed.

Jorge looked down at his shirt, which was torn and splattered with blood. "Yeah, that would explain it," he agreed. "Either way, seems like you haven't had any problems here."

"Nothing to speak of," Mike replied.

Jorge nodded his understanding. There was a palpable pause.

"Seems like there's something on your mind ..." Mike proposed.

"Well ... I don't want this to come out the wrong way, but—"

"How are we making this work?" Mike finished for him.

"Yeah."

"We set our intention," Mike said. "We put it out there in the universe, and then we live our lives as if the world we hope for already exists. Are you familiar with the quantum field and the observer effect?"

"What do you think?" Jorge replied sarcastically. "Do I look like I'm familiar with the quantum field?"

"Well, the short story is, you can choose to live by what's called the Newtonian model of reality, i.e., it happens to you, or you can live by the quantum model, which suggests we can use our own energy to manipulate the energy field around us and actually build the world we want. In a very real way, we can actually manipulate the energy of the universe to build our own reality."

"That sounds fucking *crazy*," Jorge surmised.

Mike laughed. "Hey, I don't disagree with you,

but how else can you explain all this? We're in the middle of what, by all reliable accounts, can only be described as the apocalypse, and I've got a guy down the street teaching knitting."

"But you still eat people," Jorge added.

"That is true," Mike acquiesced. "But we don't kill people for food. We eat only those who have expired naturally—and even that may be over soon."

"What do you mean?"

Mike tapped a finger on the countertop for a moment, as if he were trying to decide whether to continue. "We have the second generation of the vaccine. The one that's supposed to reverse what the first one did."

"Sounds like you're putting a lot of faith in that."

"I've already seen the result," Mike stated. "In the quantum field."

"What about in the normal field?"

"We administered the first dozen doses around midnight. Once we see the effect of those, we'll move on to the others."

"Where are they at? The ones who took the vaccine?"

"After they took their dose, they went on a vision quest into the woods, just past the bridge where you came into town. They'll return to us with news of their transformation."

"What if it's luck?" Jorge asked.

"What do you mean?"

"All this. What if it's all just luck?"

Mike shrugged. "Who can say how the field works? Perhaps it *is* just luck, but the result's still the same."

"Until your luck runs out."

Mike smiled. "Stay for lunch," he said. "We do some things with meat here you won't believe."

"All tastes the same, don't it?" Jorge asked.

"It's more about the ritual than anything else. Staying a little closer to being human."

Jorge checked his watch. "Look, I just need to check in on whoever this guy is the King's interested in."

"You're talking about Fred."

"If you say so. He didn't give me a name," Jorge said. "But I've got to get eyes-on. See for myself he's in one piece."

"We can do that," Mike affirmed. "Just give me a minute to lock up, and I'll take you down the way."

"Lock up?" Jorge said. "I'm not trying to be a dick, but I thought you were building the perfect society here? Living in the field and all."

"That's the thing about getting closer to being human," Mike said. "Humans want to do human things. Like lie and steal."

Cotton slowed his walk about fifty meters from the man in the road and did a quick survey. The man was geared up, like Harris's men had been when they'd hit him at the house, but this guy was different. Cotton could tell he was wearing a pretty solid Ferro Concepts FCPC Multicam plate carrier, and it had clearly seen some use. His rifle was also well configured, with an old school ACOG sight, and Cotton had the distinct sense the man knew how to use it.

"Peel off here," Cotton said to Jean.

She nodded and stopped, then took a knee. This helped to minimize how much of a target she could present and would also provide her with a stable shooting position if she needed it.

Cotton continued walking and pulled his sling tight to secure his rifle to his body before holding up both hands. He wanted to make damn sure this man knew he wasn't a threat, or at least that he didn't intend to be.

The man in the road also raised his hands.

Cotton walked another forty meters and then stopped, ten meters from the man in the road. He could see an identification patch on his plate carrier. On it was an eagle, globe, and anchor; the signifying mark of the United States Marine Corps. Beside it was the name 'Sgt. Maj. Wikham.'

"Sergeant Major," Cotton said with a smile.

Sergeant Major Wikham looked around and then returned his focus back to Cotton. "Friends call me Wik," he said. "What should I call you?"

"Cotton," he replied. "I was with 1/8 back in the day."

Wik smiled. "No shit? I was with 1/8, back when I was a Gunny. What did you do after?"

"SEALs," Cotton replied.

"I won't hold it against you," Wik responded jovially. "What are you doing out here, Cotton? With them?"

"Just tryin' to get where I'm going," Cotton replied. "With my daughter. We ran into a little trouble outside of Round Rock, and these people helped us out."

"They former military?" Wik asked.

"They are."

Wik nodded.

"You with FPAR?" Cotton asked.

"It's not that simple anymore," Wik said. "Used to be, but now it's turned into something else."

"How do you mean?"

Wik tapped the stock of his rifle and then let out a breath. "Can't say much considering your current affiliation," he said, indicating Cotton's traveling partners. "But it's pretty obvious at this point the Federal Government is no longer a threat."

"Because it doesn't exist," Cotton stated.

"That's right. But the Russians are starting to move south."

"Shit."

"And they're not going to stop at the Dakotas. They want it all, specifically the oil fields. That means they're coming here, and sooner than we might think."

"What about the Chinese? Last I heard, they were off the coast of California."

"Not anymore. They're in California now. Took San Francisco real fast and … Well, there wasn't much of anyone left in Los Angeles to push back. They kept going after that, but we stopped them at the Rockies. They weren't ready for that; for the real mountain warfare stuff."

"'We?'" Cotton asked.

Wik looked at Cotton hard for a moment. "Some

of us still believe in a future," he said doggedly. "Even if everyone else has given up."

Cotton furrowed his brow and felt his neck tighten. He easily recognized the insinuation. "You don't know me," he said sternly.

"I know enough. I know you're runnin' with them," Wik said, nodding to the caravan. "And by now, I know the look of a man who's just trying to get out."

Cotton took a breath and calmed himself. This wasn't the time or place to get in a fight over his ego. "Be that as it may," he said, "all I want to know is if you're going to let us pass, or if we're going to have a problem here."

Wik sensed he might have pushed too far. He didn't know a thing about this man, and he wondered if he would be doing any different to Cotton if his daughter was still around.

"Look," Wik said. "I apologize. I shouldn't have said that shit."

"Don't bother me none."

"Then you're a better man than I am," Wik replied with a smirk. "But yeah, you can pass. We're not looking to get in any fights we can avoid."

"So, you're going, then?" Cotton asked. "North? To get in a fight there? Think you've got a chance?"

"Didn't you ever think about how much shit we got into in Afghanistan? How many knock-down, drag-out fights?" Wik asked, correctly assuming Cotton had served there, just as he had. "Did you ever actually look at how much money we spent trying to take down a nation of fucking goat herders?"

Cotton couldn't help but laugh at that. He knew the numbers. "We're not goat herders," he said.

"Damn right," Wik said assuredly. "We just came out of two decades of war, the pandemic, and now these fucking cannibals. Now Ivan and his buddies want to come and fuck with us on our own front porch? I think not. The Reds are about to get a goddamn masterclass in guerrilla warfare. This is gonna make Afghanistan look like the welcome wagon."

"Tell me the truth," Cotton said, looking Wik dead in the eye. "All dick-swinging aside. Do you really have a chance?"

Wik held his gaze. "Yes."

Cotton looked down at the ground and then back to his daughter.

"Some of the guys we were fighting over there were her age," Wik said. Cotton shot him a dirty look. "You know it's true."

"Doesn't mean I liked it."

"You can't protect her forever," Wik said. "At some point, she's going to have to fight for her own future—and it looks to me she's no stranger to fighting."

"You're not wrong," Cotton said, "but I also know what I have to do as a father, which is to get her as far away from this shit as possible. We'll work out the rest later."

"Understood," Wik said with a nod. "As long as you remember tomorrow eventually becomes today."

Wik turned and began walking down the road, then stopped.

"You on the net?" Wik called back.

"I am."

"Whiskey-two-nine," Wik said. "Frequency 145.1900. You can find me there at dusk and dawn. Fifteen minutes each day."

"You won't hear from me," Cotton said as he turned and walked back to where Jean was holding position on the road.

"We'll see."

Cotton approached the second vehicle in the line and found Roland waiting for him.

"Looked like you two were enjoying old home week," Roland said sarcastically.

"Former Marine," Cotton said. "He was with 1/8."

"How about now?" Roland asked. "He gonna let us pass?"

Cotton thought for a moment about everything Wik had told him and made a conscious decision not to pass that information on to Roland.

"Yeah, we can pass."

As the rest of the convoy fired their engines back up, Cotton and Jean took their places back in the truck with April.

"What happened?" April asked.

Cotton looked at her for a moment. He knew he still couldn't fully trust the woman, but he also understood that if he was ever going to, that trust had to start somewhere.

"They were FPAR," Cotton said. "But they didn't care about us. They're heading north to stop the Russians."

"Holy shit!" April nearly shouted. Cotton had briefed Jean on the walk back to the vehicles, so the girl remained stoic. "It's really happening?"

"Yes, it is," Cotton said, and he leaned in closer to her and lowered his voice. "But we need to keep this in the circle. No one else knows. Do you understand?"

There was hesitation in April's eyes, and Cotton could tell she was conflicted, but only for a brief moment.

"Okay," April said. "I get it."

CHAPTER 2

Jorge followed Mike down a winding rock path toward what looked like a run-down barn on the outskirts of Tow. Parked in front of the structure was a perfectly restored 1948 DeSoto sedan. Jorge stopped in front of it and looked incredulously at Mike.

"Is this what I think it is?"

Mike smiled. "It is. Fred's little side project."

"Does this thing run?"

"You bet your ass it does." Jorge turned to his left to see a woman standing just inside the barn door. "And it'll wipe the floor with that Toyota you drove in here."

That wasn't an accident, Jorge immediately

thought to himself. *Whoever this woman is, she wants me to know she was watching me.*

"*This,*" Mike said, "is Fred."

"Frederique," the woman said. "If you need the whole name. But I go by Fred."

Jorge examined her for a moment, understanding Mike had played him for the fool; not a lot, but enough to be annoying. This woman was quite a bit older than him, most likely in her late fifties, and was heavyset, with wild gray hair that seemed to travel in every possible direction. She wore thick, coke bottle glasses and overalls. Despite the ensemble, he could see that Fred took great care in her appearance. She also did not appear to be overweight, but rather as if she had spent her life moving car engines or farm equipment. She was precisely what Jorge imagined a woman working the fields in the Soviet Union would have looked like.

"I'm Jorge," he said. "Sorry, the King led me to believe you were a man."

Fred smiled. "He tends to do that. Seems to think I'm some kind of national treasure because I can change a light bulb."

"You did this?" Jorge asked, indicating the DeSoto.

Fred nodded. "After everything went to shit, too.

So, maybe I *am* something special. EMP won't take it out, either. Pre-1984."

"Yeah," Jorge said slowly. "I remember hearing about that once." He thought about it a little more. "Wait—you think an EMP's coming?"

"I think *a lot's* coming," Fred said. "But what I think and what's actually going to happen are two very different things."

"You good with him?" Mike asked. "Reginald's teaching a knitting class. I want to break me off some of that."

Fred laughed. "Yeah, go to your knitting class," she replied with a wave.

Without another moment wasted, Mike walked back down the rock path, and within a minute, he was out of sight.

Fred's face changed, lines of concern replacing her ready smile. Her eyes bored holes in Jorge. "You armed?"

The question caught Jorge off guard. "No. They made me leave my gun at the truck. Why?"

"Because I think something bad is about to happen."

. . .

Jorge stood in silence as Fred adjusted some knobs on what appeared to be a pretty impressive HAM radio set. While he'd had no problems with military issue communications gear and even some of the more high-speed stuff Delta had used, the whole HAM radio thing had eluded him. Part of the reason for this was he didn't really care. So far, satellite phones still worked because they were run by companies based overseas, so the complete destruction of the United States hadn't actually affected their ability to function.

"It started an hour ago." Fred hit a switch that ported the audio from her headphones over to a small speaker.

A dull, ringing noise emanated from the speaker.

"What am I listening to?" Jorge asked.

"Nothing," Fred said. "That's the point. What you're hearing is a continuous signal. That isn't supposed to happen on HAM radio. It should be people clicking in and out of the net, not a freakin' dial tone!"

"Okay. You've gotta work with me here a little bit," Jorge said. "I'm a trigger puller, not a comms guy. What does it mean?"

"It means the station that usually runs this frequency is down."

"Which station is that?"

"Houston. Seems as though their entire communications infrastructure has crashed."

"How does something like that happen?"

"I was hoping you could tell me. You're the one out there. I just sit in this barn all day."

"I know about as much about the ins and outs of Houston as you do."

"There's this, too," Fred said, reaching across the desk to hit the play button on an old school recorder. It crackled for a moment with background noise and then a voice spoke.

"Calling all stations on the net. Cypress Mill has fallen."

"I record everything that comes out of Cypress Mill and Oatmeal," Fred explained. "That came through an hour ago."

"Wait a minute," Jorge said, leaning forward. "Play that again."

Fred hit the rewind button and then re-played the message.

"I know that voice," Jorge said emphatically. "I'm pretty sure that's June Kennedy."

"You know her?" Fred asked.

"She's kind of the den mother at Cypress Mill,

but I have no idea why she'd be on the net saying something like that."

"Can't be a coincidence, can it? Houston Station is out for the count," Fred said, "and now this woman is saying Cypress Mill has also fallen. And I can't raise a signal out of Oatmeal to save my life."

"No morning report?" Jorge asked.

"Nothing," Fred confirmed. "It's like it doesn't exist anymore."

Jorge looked around the barn, and his eyes settled on what looked like a class photo from Texas A&M University. "You went to A&M?" he asked.

Fred looked at the photo. "No, I went to Oxford. I was a Professor of Mathematics at A&M."

"Shit," Jorge groused.

"Tell me about it. There aren't many things more useless in this new world than a math degree."

"No, it's not that. I was looking around for something that would confirm you're just some nut in a barn and I shouldn't be worried about all this."

"Sorry to disappoint," Fred replied. "Won the Fields medal and everything." She could see by Jorge's blank expression that the reference meant nothing to him. "For a mathematician, it makes me like the SEAL who killed Bin Laden."

. . .

Brian checked his watch. Jorge had been gone for nearly an hour. Out of respect for the town rules, he had agreed to lock their guns in the truck's security box and let Jorge depart with the keys. It seemed like a pretty dumb-ass idea to Brian, but he also understood they had to play it cool with the locals to check this errand off their list and get home, wherever that might end up being.

He was also beginning to realize it had been quite a while since he'd eaten last, and he decided it was probably necessary to see what the town had to offer in the way of sustenance before they got back on the road. In the meantime, he'd been sitting in the back of the truck, reading a well-worn copy of *Titus Andronicus* that he kept in his hip pocket to distract himself from his hunger.

Truth be told, Brian didn't understand even ten percent of the text, but he had found that by reading and re-reading it repeatedly over the past year, it was starting to make sense. In his other hip pocket, he also had a dictionary, which he could use to look up some of the words he didn't know.

Brian stopped scanning the page. His peripheral vision had picked up something out near the tree line. He looked up, and his eyes settled on a young woman standing just beyond the trees. She wore a summer dress and had long blonde hair. She sure wasn't hard to look at, and she seemed to be looking at him.

Brian closed the book and slid it back into his pocket as he stood up in the truck bed. He held his hand over his eyes to shield them from the sun. The woman wasn't saying or doing anything; she was just standing there, staring at him. She also looked weirdly fit. It occurred to Brian that this was a strange thought to have, but her skin was almost bright pink and veins stood out in bold relief on her arms and neck. There was also something strange about her eyes. She was too far away for Brian to see clearly what it was, but there was something there.

Something *wrong*.

He watched as her lips slowly pulled back from her teeth, and he could hear her from across the field. She was growling.

"What the hell?" Brian muttered.

She started running.

She was fast, much faster than Brian would have imagined a woman her size could be. There was something different about how she was running, almost animal-like, as if she were gliding across the ground. She had been about two hundred yards away when she was standing by the trees but was already closing the gap between the two of them—and fast.

"Hey there!" Brian shouted. "You better stop right now, lady!"

Not only did the woman not stop, she seemed to be picking up speed.

The guns were still locked in the security trunk. Brian looked down at the truck bed and saw a single tire iron wedged in behind a net bag. He reached down and snatched it up. The woman was almost to the truck. He had been right; there *was* something wrong with her eyes.

They were black. Solid black.

"Stop!" Brian shouted again, the panic obvious in his voice this time.

Then the woman did something beyond belief. She was still several feet from the truck when she launched herself from the ground and traveled through the air, straight toward Brian.

If Brian had thought about it, if he had let the emotional part of his brain make the decision, he probably would not have taken the action he did. Instead, primal reflexes took over, and he swung the tire iron as hard as he could, connecting with the side of the woman's face as she lunged for him.

In that moment, he looked into those coal black

eyes and knew there was nothing human left within her. She had become some sort of animal.

There was an audible *crack* as the tire iron crushed the side of the woman's skull and her body twisted in midair, crashing into the truck bed beside Brian. In a moment, she was on him. It happened so fast and was in such stark contradiction to what his brain thought should be happening that Brian couldn't process the development in time.

He felt himself slam into the bed of the truck and drop the tire iron, one of the frenzied woman's hands gripping his arm and the other on his throat. Her right eye bulged from its socket where the tire iron had hit her and spit flew from her mouth as she throttled him and growled.

The woman was impossibly strong. That was the only thought that kept cycling through Brian's head as he desperately fought to keep her off of him. How was she so strong?

Finally, consciousness caught up and Brian reached for the knife in its sheath on his belt. He drew it, shoved the woman as hard as he could away from him, and drove the blade into her ribs.

The wound didn't even slow her down. This time, she didn't bother trying to break him with her hands; instead, she lunged straight for his throat with her teeth, dragging the knife and Brian's knife hand with her. Brian turned quickly and shoulder-checked her hard enough to buy the moment he needed to retrieve his knife and strike again. This time, he didn't expect a single blow to do the job; he threw overhand strike after overhand strike until she finally withdrew and fell over the side of the truck and into the dirt.

Brian quickly switched the knife to his left hand and snatched the tire iron back up with his right. He was ready for the next round if that was what it took, determined the girl wouldn't be getting a round three.

The bloodied woman just sat in the dirt. Brian was breathing like a racehorse and could feel his heart pounding out of his chest. The woman turned her head and looked at him. She was bleeding from at least a half dozen wounds, and there was something about the look in her eyes that told him she knew she was beaten. He had been wrong. She wasn't just an animal.

Slowly, she stood up and limped away, heading back for the tree line she had emerged from, leaving a trail of blood in her wake.

In one horrifying instant, Brian realized the woman probably wasn't alone. He scrambled over the edge of the truck, hit the ground, and ran past the empty greeter's stool and over the bridge that led into Tow.

"We need to bring Mike in on this," Jorge said after considering the situation they appeared to be in, even if he wasn't sure just what that situation actually was.

Fred shook her head. "Won't do any good."

"Let me guess ..."

"Leave it to the field," Fred confirmed. "By the way, I'm the only person in this town who *actually* understands quantum theory, and I know this is a load of shit."

"So, why are you here?" Jorge asked. "If you don't believe in all their hippy bullshit, why do you stay?"

"The people here let me do what I want," Fred said with a shrug. "And every day I'm here is another day I can pretend the world didn't go to shit and we're not all eating human flesh."

"But it did, and you are."

Fred's eyes softened. "I just ... I need this. I need the illusion. Maybe the same way Tow needs the quantum field. You know, to get me through one day to the next."

"Well, sorry to have to tell you, but I think your days just ran out. We need to move on this."

"It won't matter. You can tell them all you want. The people here won't do anything."

"Hey! I need help!"

Jorge turned to the barn door, toward the sound of the screaming voice outside.

It was Brian.

Jorge stepped outside. "Hey!" he shouted, waving Brian down as the young man sprinted past the barn on the rock path.

Brian came to a stop so quickly, he almost went ass over teakettle. As he came into focus, Jorge could see he was covered in blood.

"*Jesus!*" the boy shouted, barely able to catch his breath. "We have a real problem, Jorge!"

"No kidding," Jorge confirmed. "What the hell happened to you?"

Brian relayed his story as Fred joined them, taking it all in. By the time he'd finished speaking, she was white with shock.

"That's Celeste," she said quietly.

"You know her?" Brian asked.

"I do," Fred replied, her eyes darting back and

forth as if searching for something. "She was part of the group that took the Gen 2 Pandemify and walked out into the woods."

It took Jorge a moment to process what she was implying. "You think the vaccine did this?"

"Look what the last one did," Fred said skeptically. "You tell me."

"Wait a minute," Brian interjected. "You said she was with a group? There's *more* of them?"

"Twelve in total," Fred said. "*Shit*. They're about to vaccinate a dozen more after the knitting class."

"We need to get the hell out of here!" Brian shouted. "We can't take on that many of those things!"

Jorge looked to where an old axe was wedged into a stump beside a pile of firewood. He walked to it and pulled it free.

"He's right," Jorge said. "We can't stay here, not if there's two dozen of them. We need to get back to the truck and get our guns."

"We'd be walking right into them," Brian said. "I'd bet my last nickel she was heading back into the woods to re-group."

"I think I'd make the same bet," Fred said quietly.

Jorge could see her eyes were locked on the trail

Brian had just come racing down. He turned and saw what she was looking at. There were roughly a dozen figures walking down the rock trail. Right away, he identified the one who had attacked Brian. The side of her face was caved in, her gait was more of a stumble, and she was bleeding from several stab wounds. Jorge didn't understand how she was staying upright.

He looked around and then back to Fred. "Get in the car, now!" he commanded.

Fred didn't hesitate. She understood what was happening. She opened the door to the DeSoto, got inside, and locked it.

By now, the black-eyed cannibals had spotted them and broken into a run.

"We have to fight!" Jorge said. "There's no time to run."

With the cannibals only a few dozen feet away, he could see Brian was scared, but he also knew the young man wouldn't cut and run. He could count on him.

Jorge calculated their speed without even thinking about it, stepped forward as the horde drew close, took a sideways swing with the axe, and found the ribs of the first one in line.

Brian went to work as well, this time keeping his

calm as best he could, enough to make precision strikes. In a split second, he understood blows to the head or the knees were his best bet; either switch off the command center or hobble them.

Jorge threw a kick into the torso of his first victim, enough to let him pull the axe free. He felt another cannibal jump on his back and could feel its hot breath on the side of his throat. He slammed his head back, and it made violent contact with his attacker's face, significant enough to jar the cannibal loose from his back.

He spun and, in one fluid motion, brought the axe down on the cannibal's head, splitting it in two.

Fred braced herself against the front seat of the old car as two of the black-eyed cannibals leapt on the hood and began slamming their fists into the windshield. The thick glass held, but she knew it wouldn't for long. She could see Jorge and the boy were holding their own, but there were just too many attackers. Their time was going to run out.

She reached for the glove box and popped it open, grasped beneath some paperwork inside, and pulled out a .38 Special she had hidden in there long ago. Bringing it up to eye level, Fred drew the hammer back and pulled the trigger.

The first round she fired went right where she had intended: between the eyes of the closest black-eyed cannibals. Her vision blurred and her ears were instantly ringing from the sound of the revolver firing in such an enclosed space, but she overcame it, lined her front sight up with the second cannibal, and executed him at point blank range, too.

Fred grabbed the door handle and opened it, but mis-timed her exit and tumbled to the ground. Her equilibrium was disrupted from the gunfire in the car. Before she fully understood what was happening, another of the cannibals was on top of her, jaws snapping as he went directly for her face.

He's actually trying to eat my face! Fred thought in a moment of sheer panic.

She punched the .38 forward like it was an extension of her fist, directly into her attacker's mouth. A single trigger pull blew out the back of the cannibal's head and his body went limp, collapsing on top of her.

. . .

Jorge pivoted into his axe swing like a Major League baseball player and slammed it into the side of the black-eyed cannibal's head.

Something was drawing the horde's attention away from him. He'd heard the gunshots but hoped to hell Fred had the sense to stay in the car and not try to be a hero.

Brian had made short work of two cannibals and heard another gunshot. He turned and saw Fred walking toward them, shooting another of the attacking cannibals in the head.

Jorge stopped and looked around. He slowed his breathing. The horde were all dead.

All except one.

Brian stood with his boot on Celeste's throat, the girl who had first attacked him. He looked unsure.

Jorge made eye contact with Fred. "I thought you weren't supposed to have guns here?"

"We're also not supposed to have extras from 28 *Days Later*," Fred replied flippantly. Then her eyes found Celeste, writhing on the ground beneath Brian's boot. "Let her up," she said.

"Are you nuts?" Brian asked. "She'll chew your damn face off!"

Fred walked to within a few feet of where Brian stood. "Let her up," she repeated. "I'll do it."

"You sure about this?" Jorge asked.

"I know her," Fred replied. "It should be someone she knows."

Jorge looked at Brian and nodded.

Brian stepped back, removing his boot from Celeste's throat. The woman quickly stumbled to her feet, much quicker than anyone would have expected based on the sheer amount of trauma that had been inflicted upon her. She turned to Fred and snarled, baring her bloody and broken teeth.

"I'm sorry, sweet girl," Fred said as she raised the .38 and pointed it at Celeste. There were tears in her eyes. "You didn't deserve this."

She pulled the trigger, and the gunshot whipped Celeste's head back. Her body collapsed.

Jorge reached out and took the gun from Fred's shaking hand. "I'm sorry," he said. "But we have to move. We got lucky here. If there's more of them, we probably won't get off so easy."

His words almost prophetic, the three heard a scream in the distance. Fred turned and looked toward the sound.

"The others," she said. "They must have turned. How could it have happened so fast?"

"We can't help them!" Jorge insisted. "There's

only one play here. We have to get the hell out, *now!*"

"We can't just leave them!" Fred insisted. "It's inhuman!"

"We're not human!" Jorge shouted. "And if you want to survive you need to come to grips with that."

For a moment, Fred didn't respond, but eventually she nodded. She understood. Even if she didn't like it, she knew the truth behind Jorge's words.

Sheila opened her eyes and looked up at the ceiling. There was still light coming through the bars on the armory's single window; not much, admittedly, but enough for her to know it was still daytime. She had no idea how long she had been out; it could have been minutes, hours, or days. Being a cannibal, she knew she could go days without eating, so hunger pangs wouldn't be a useful tool for determining how much time had passed.

She sat up and put her fingers to her ears. They were sore, but there was no acute pain. She rubbed them gently, and her fingers came away with dried blood. At least she wasn't bleeding anymore. That was something.

Slowly, Sheila worked her way to standing. Her whole body hurt, no doubt the aftereffects of an adrenaline dump from running and fighting. She looked around the room and saw that, sure enough, she had what seemed like an unlimited supply of weapons and ammunition. She supposed that was something.

Then she had a horrifying thought.

"No," she said quietly, reaching out to test the door.

Nothing. It was locked from the outside.

"*No!*"

Sheila took a step back from the door and slowed her breathing down. She knew she had to stay calm. There was no way to unlock the armory from the inside. Why would there be? Why would anyone be dumb enough to lock themselves in the armory?

She wasn't getting out that door unless someone opened it from the hallway. There were explosives in the room, but they wouldn't do her much good. Even if Sheila knew how to use them, trying to breach the door with anything stronger than a crowbar would most likely kill her in the process.

She walked to the window and examined the bars that had been installed there. They were sunk deep into the concrete wall. Sawing through them was a possibility, but who knew how long that would take?

I could starve in here, Sheila thought to herself. It had been about forty-eight hours since she last ate, assuming she hadn't been out for more than a day. If she had, it was possible there were only hours remaining before she would begin to consume herself from the inside.

She had seen the bodies of cannibals who went out that way. It was nothing she wanted, a really bad way to go.

Across the room was a stack of bins, and opening them up, she began to search for the handsaw she knew was there. She remembered it from a while back, when she had been helping to organize the armory. Finally, she found it, pulling the small tool out of its bin.

Sheila looked at it for a moment. It was too small to work through the bars on the window. She looked down to her left arm. It was just the right size to pass through muscle and bone.

Sheila knew this had happened before, when a cannibal was trapped or was in a scenario where they couldn't get food. True self-cannibalism. She knew she could get by without her left arm below the elbow. It was a fairly simple solution that would probably keep her alive for at least a week, maybe even more.

But what would it achieve? What if no one came? What if they had all been killed by whatever those things outside were, and no one was coming for her? Could cannibals become dehydrated enough to die? They seemed to need less water than humans, but no one had ever tested how long they could really go without it.

"I could drink my own blood," she said to herself.

Amongst all the unknowns, Sheila did know one thing: she would fight to her last breath. If someone did finally come and find her dead torso on the floor, if they knew nothing else, they would know she had not given up.

"Walk into the sun. Find me in the woods."

Sheila jumped. It was the voice again, the one from after she had fired the shotgun, but it wasn't coming from anywhere outside. It was coming from inside her own head.

"Who the hell is that?" she shouted. She could tell her hearing was severely damaged; even her own voice sounded like it was underwater. "Can you hear me?"

"Walk together. We are stronger together."

"You can't hear me," Sheila said quietly. "But I can hear *you*."

Then Sheila gasped as she felt the pain, like a knife being driven into her stomach.

"*No*," she whimpered and dropped to her knees. "It's too soon!"

Then there was another pain, and another, and another. She stumbled across the concrete floor to the workbench and pulled herself to her feet. With sudden realization, a bizarre clarity brought on by the pain, Sheila turned to where the coffeepot sat on a shelf. She made sure it was plugged in, pulled the pot off the burner, and flipped the switch. It was another ridiculous thing cannibals did; just like with alcohol, they still drank coffee. Even though they technically couldn't taste it, they could still sense the acidity in their mouths.

Sheila didn't know how hot that burner got, but she hoped to hell it was hot enough to cauterize a wound.

Sheila reached down and pulled off her belt, then wrapped it around her left arm above the elbow and cinched it as tight as it would go. She opened up the vice on the workbench and set her forearm in it at the highest point, just below the elbow. She tightened it down until it felt like her arm would break from the pressure.

The hunger pangs kept coming, faster and more intense each time.

"You *will not* die like this!" she shouted, and then she took the tail end of the thick leather belt and bit down on it as hard as she could.

CHAPTER 3

THE CONVOY SLOWED to a stop several hundred feet down the road from the main entrance to Cypress Mill, and Cotton listened to the chatter on the net between Roland Reese and Randall Eisler.

"*Something ain't right,*" Randall Eisler said.

There was a pause for a moment and then Roland came back. "*I'm on binos. There's a dead man on top of that semi. See if you can confirm.*"

Another pause.

"*Confirmed,*" Randall Eisler came back. "*Pretty sure that's one of mine. Hard to tell from here.*"

The convoy had stopped at a bend in the road, where it would most likely not be seen by anyone within the main gate. Both Randall Eisler and Roland knew that moving forward without understanding what they were about to walk into could be suicide.

"Want to try to raise them again?" Roland asked.

"Negative," Randall Eisler replied. *"At this point, the only thing that will achieve is giving us away."* There was a pause on the line. *"We need to send a recce into the woods and come out around the rear gate. See if they can get eyes-on."*

"Roger that," Roland replied. *"Cotton, get on the line."*

"Shit," Cotton said with a sigh. He knew where this was going. "This is Cotton."

"You're the recon guy," Roland said. *"We both know it. Can you do this for us?"*

Cotton hesitated, then keyed the mic. "Yeah, I can do it."

"Do you need a second?" Roland asked.

Cotton thought about it. "No. Singleton's my thing, you know that. I'll get it done, come out the front, and guide you in."

"Roger that," Roland came back. *"But don't take any chances. You always had a hard time with the concept of recon work. Mainly, do not engage."*

Cotton laughed. "There must have been a misprint in my manual," he replied and then set the radio back on its hook.

"You're going in there?" April asked. "Alone?"

"Only way to find out what happened here so we can get back on the road."

Cotton stepped out of the vehicle. He pulled his rifle sling loose from the bands that had been securing it for vehicle operations and looped the weapon back around his body. He thought briefly about applying some camouflage but then decided against it. Hopefully this wouldn't take long, and the pain in the ass that was trying to remove camo paint from his face wasn't worth it.

"What should I do?" Jean asked.

"Hold fast," Cotton replied. "And keep your head on a swivel. I'll be back."

It was deathly quiet. Quiet in a way the woods shouldn't be.

Cotton moved furtively through the trees, doing his best to stay hidden but knowing he was sacrificing some degree of fieldcraft for speed. While he didn't want to be sloppy, he also didn't want the recce to take all day.

He moved in a wide loop around the edge of the woods, on a bearing he knew should bring him out on the other side of the town. While Cotton had never been to Cypress Mill, knowing the general size of the place and that there was an entry point on the other side, it was reasonable to think he would eventually hit it.

He stopped suddenly and raised his weapon, keeping his line of sight above the EOTech reticle. If a target presented itself, he would 'ready up' and execute, but so far, he hadn't seen anything.

He had, however, *smelled* something.

He smelled urine. More specifically, *human* urine. Someone had been out pissing in the woods.

Cotton looked around and saw the broken branches and disturbed foliage left behind by the person who'd emptied their bladder. He slowly flicked off the safety on his DDM4 and moved forward in the direction the tracking signs led him.

He stopped again. The first thing that caught his eyes was the blood on a tree about ten feet ahead of him. It wasn't just a little; the trunk looked as if it had been spray-painted dark red. To create that much spray, someone must have had their carotid artery severed.

Then his eyes went to the ground and he saw the source of the blood.

Cotton whipped his head around but saw nothing. There was no one. Whoever—or *whatever*—had done this was long gone, or at least he hoped to hell they were. The last thing he needed was to be getting into an uneven gunfight in the middle of these woods.

He looked down at the source of the blood, and it took his brain a moment to process what he was seeing. It was a man—or at least he thought it was. The body had been torn to shreds in a way Cotton had never seen before, and the head was cracked wide open. He kept his eyes fixed on the carnage for a moment longer than he would have liked and then snapped out of it.

Whatever had happened here, it had been over for quite a while. The blood was more brown and tacky to the touch, not red and slick like it might have been directly in the aftermath.

Cotton tightened his grip on the rifle and moved forward through the path to the tree line. Beyond this, he could see a large open field and, further beyond, the rear gate into Cypress Mill. It looked to be just a simple cattle fence.

Not exactly Fort Knox.

Then Cotton spotted what appeared to be bodies in the field. From the looks of things, there were over a dozen of them, and just like the man at the base of the tree back there, the corpses were shredded.

Cotton slowed down as he hit the edge of the woods and took a knee. He snapped up the magnifier behind his weapon sight and looked through it, panning the field to get a closer look at what lay between him and the town.

He saw no signs of any aggressor, just the mangled bodies. Whoever had killed them was fast and strong; fast enough to run these men down before they could make it to the town. There was no way they had used tools or machinery to do all of this because it wouldn't have been fast enough. And the lack of precision to the injuries were inconsistent with weapons being used.

No, whoever had done this had used their bare hands.

Cotton took a closer look at the field and found what he was looking for: bloodstains and drag marks. To him, it looked like the poor bastards had taken down at least a handful of their attackers, but those bodies had then been removed.

This was bad. It was bad, and he knew it. Whoever had done this was either long gone or waiting to bushwhack him the moment he stepped out in the open.

Cotton looked around the field and saw no better option than simply walking straight through it.

He keyed the radio in his chest rig and spoke quietly. "I'm getting ready to enter through the rear. There's sign of a fight here. Bodies everywhere. Don't come in, no matter what you hear. I'll exit the front to get you. Going radio silent."

Exactly as requested, there was no reply.

He re-checked all of his gear as he stood in the tree line. He performed a brass check on the AR, then let it hang and did the same thing on his Glock 17 sidearm.

Cotton let out a breath and then broke from the trees.

The rear gate wasn't much to speak of, and Cotton clambered over it with ease.

The field had been a slaughter. Sure enough, there were nearly two dozen bodies strewn across it, each one more mangled than the next.

His boots hit the pavement and he stopped. He looked around and listened.

There was nothing. Not a sound.

He moved forward and saw a large structure to his left that looked like some kind of old warehouse. The door was slid open, and a blood trail ran into the street from the inside.

Cotton moved in a wide loop around the door and activated the DDM4's SureFire light. It wouldn't give away his position standing out in the daylight, but it would illuminate the inside of the warehouse just fine. He kept his distance as he panned the inside with the light, and he found just what he'd imagined he might: more mangled bodies, most with the heads missing. There were at least a half dozen of them.

He turned away from the warehouse and moved down Main Street, staying close to the buildings on his left. Normally, Cotton wouldn't have left an uncleared structure in his wake, but he hadn't come to Cypress Mill to put on a CQB clinic. All he had to do was confirm there were no active threats in the area and then open the front gate. Once he'd done that and had some backup, they could take the time to clear the town building by building.

Main Street took a lazy turn to the right, and Cotton followed it as it opened up into the center of the town. He slowed down and lowered his rifle.

"*Jesus*," he gasped.

The bodies were everywhere. He assumed this was the place where the people of Cypress Mill had made their stand, and it had not been a successful one. Something about the scene was different, though. There was a scattering of mangled bodies, but the majority were still whole.

At the other end of the massacre, Cotton could see the road that led through the front gate and past the jack-knifed semi. That was where he needed to go.

He just had to walk through this killing field to get there.

Sheila sat slumped against the cold brick wall. She stared at what remained of her left arm in the vice. She'd looked directly at the stump when she'd cauterized it using the burner on the coffee maker, but she hadn't directly inspected it since then. She knew at a certain point she would likely need some sort of medical attention. Even with the accelerated healing that came with being a cannibal, there was still a risk of infection setting in.

She let out a breath and looked down at her left arm. It didn't look the way she'd thought it would—or, rather, it didn't cause the emotional output she had expected it might. There was no emotion attached to it; it was just something she'd had to do to survive.

Like so many other things she had done.

For a moment, Sheila wondered where Jorge was. Had what happened in Oatmeal happened anywhere else, like where he was in Cypress Mill? Had she been too hard on him when he'd come with that kid to check in?

No, how was she *supposed* to react? After not seeing or hearing from him for months, he suddenly just appears out of the blue, and she's supposed to pretend nothing ever happened? She's supposed to act like he hadn't told her what he did? She also wondered if she'd handled that poorly.

It was true that Sheila had taken the collapse of civilization better than most. Hell, life post-collapse wasn't that much different than an average Tuesday in the MC. Even so, at least back then, you had the option of getting out if you decided you'd had enough, not that she ever would. Even though, as a woman, she was never going to be a 'full patch' member of the Louisiana Reavers Motorcycle Club, Sheila was as close as any woman would ever get.

But sometimes she wished Jorge had just kept his big mouth shut.

"*I took that shot that killed the President, not Roland,*" he'd said to her while they were laying in bed.

Those immortal words were shocking. It wasn't

that Sheila was a fan of the President—or even of getting the world back to 'normal,' whatever that was. She just didn't think Jorge had the right to make that decision for everyone.

She understood why he'd done it. She knew what had happened to Jorge's family because of that man, but him telling her the truth about the President's death had changed their relationship in a way that was impossible to come back from.

No, she hadn't been too hard on him. Sheila didn't know if she would have acted any differently in his position, but what he had done had changed the world forever. It wasn't far-fetched to think that his actions had directly put her in this very position.

Sheila pulled herself to her feet and caught her reflection in the mirror that was bolted to the wall. Her face was covered in blood. Her *own* blood. That same blood also covered the floor and the workbench where she had done the deed. Sheila had lost a lot of it, but so far, she still felt fully coherent and could feel her energy was coming back.

She walked to the gear locker and pulled out the first aid kit she knew was stored in there, from which she fished out a bottle of hydrogen peroxide and a roll of bandages.

This was not going to be enjoyable.

She did it quickly, or at least as quickly as she was able, dousing the wound in hydrogen peroxide. The pain took her breath away, but she stayed on task and once the liquid had stopped fizzing, she cleaned it again with water and then wrapped it carefully with the bandage. She was not one hundred percent certain it was the correct course of action, but Sheila figured it was better than nothing, and she wouldn't cause enough injury that someone with medical training wouldn't be able to fix it later. This, of course, assumed there was anyone left alive out there with medical training, and that she wasn't just going to starve to death in the armory.

Out of the corner of her eye, she caught movement in the street outside. Slowly, Sheila walked to the barred window and looked out, hoping that she was going to see someone who might be able to help her.

It was Robert. She felt her heart jump into her throat. *He's still alive! How the hell is that possible?* There had been so many of the black-eyed cannibals.

He was walking down the street outside the armory building, probably looking for her. How was she going to explain leaving him behind? She'd worry about that later. For now, she needed him to get her the hell out of this room.

"*Robert!*" she shouted. "I'm in here!"

He stopped.

Sheila sighed with relief. He had heard her. She was going to live.

Except he wasn't moving. Robert just stood in the street.

"Hey!" Sheila shouted. "I'm in the armory! Get me outta here!"

He turned his head, hesitated for a moment, and then turned a full one hundred and eighty degrees to face her.

Sheila reflexively jumped back from the window. "What the hell?"

His eyes were black. He was one of *them*, but Sheila knew for a fact he hadn't taken the Gen 2 vaccine. What was happening? Had it spread to him somehow?

But that was *impossible*—wasn't it?

Robert walked to the window and stared at her through it. Knowing it wasn't possible for him to breach the plexiglass window or the bars, Sheila walked practically nose-to-nose with her friend. There was something different about him; different from the other black-eyed cannibals she had seen that day. Robert's skin didn't have the bright pink hue the other creatures did, and there was no steam coming off of him. If anything, his skin was pale and washed out.

He coughed a few times as he was watching her, then turned and walked away.

Cotton walked slowly through the town square, careful not to step on any of the dozens of bodies that littered the ground. Once he crossed the open area, he would be back on Main Street and only a few hundred feet from Cypress Mill's front entrance.

Something caught his attention; something strange. It was similar to the deathly quiet tone of the town, but instead of sound, it was smell. There was no smell. Granted, these people were freshly dead, but people did certain things when they died, particularly when they died violently.

There should have been a smell.

Cotton stopped. Something had moved. He knew it. He'd caught traces of it out of the corner of his eye. He scanned the bodies on the ground. Nothing.

There it was again. His head snapped to the left. Something was wrong, he knew it, but his conscious brain couldn't process it. It was like the sense you get when something is out of place. You know it's out of place, but you can't put your finger on what it is or where it should have been.

Then it hit him.

No fatal wounds.

He scanned the bodies on the ground and did a second check. He was right; they were all wounded and bleeding, no question about it, but not a single one of the wounds was fatal. What had killed them all, then?

His eyes picked up movement again, but this time, he was able to isolate it. The motion came from a woman about twenty feet from him. She was pulling herself up to a seated position. His instinct was to move toward her and see if he could provide some kind of medical aid, but something else within him ordered Cotton to stop.

She opened her eyes. They were coal black.

What the hell?

Her skin was ashen, and her face was twisted with grief. Tears were flowing from her eyes and her body was shaking as she held up her hands and looked at them. Then she saw him, and her face changed. The sadness fell away and was replaced with anger. She pulled herself to her feet and began walking toward him.

"Stop," Cotton said, and then repeated himself more forcefully. "I said, *stop!*"

The woman showed no signs of slowing down, and raising his rifle, Cotton put a single round through her head, knocking her to the ground. It was a judgment call, and one he'd had to make before. Cotton didn't know this woman's history, whether she'd been a human or a cannibal, but in that moment, it didn't matter. Whatever she had been, this woman was something else now, and he didn't want to find out any more about what that thing was.

Cotton felt a hand grip his ankle with surprising force. His head whipped downward toward the threat, followed instantly by his rifle, and he put a round through the target the moment he saw the black eyes staring up at him.

They all began moving. The roughly two dozen bodies were getting up from the ground all around him.

Cotton didn't hesitate. He moved forward through the rising bodies, toward the front exit. For the moment, the bodies seemed disoriented and were moving clumsily, but he didn't expect that to last.

He was right.

Within seconds, the black-eyed creatures were running after him—and quickly gaining ground. It didn't help that he was tired and hungry and hauling gear with him. As his boots slapped the ground and he closed in on the exit, Cotton could hear the creatures coughing behind him as they ran.

He felt a hand brush against his back, fingers grasping for the straps on his chest rig as he ran. He was nearly to the front gate, maybe only twenty feet out, but the rest of the convoy was still a good hundred feet away.

He wasn't going to make it.

Cotton reached for his radio and keyed the mic. "Fire on my position!" he shouted. "Now! *Now! Do it now!*"

Roland was moving before anyone else had even processed what Cotton's radio communication was asking of them. He ran forward toward the main gate and dropped to a half-kneeling firing position, at a distance he knew he could reliably hit man-sized targets with his AR-15.

"*Holy shit,*" he muttered under his breath as he watched Cotton round the corner.

There were at least twenty people racing after him. He knew he had to trust his old teammate's judgment, but there was also something in Roland

Reese's gut that told him there was no way Cotton Wiley was going to make it out of this one.

The first volley of 5.56 rounds snapped around Cotton's head and found their targets, but not in time to stop a pair of the black-eyed things from tackling him and bringing him to the ground. Within a split second, others had joined in, and he could feel jaws snapping at his face.

Then there was a gunshot; close range, much closer than the men firing from the convoy. Then another and another, and Cotton watched a man pull one of the dead black-eyed creatures off of him.

"Welcome to the party," Harris Hawthorne said before turning and executing another black-eyed cannibal at point blank range.

Cotton didn't let conscious thought slow him down. He didn't know where Harris had come from, and he didn't really care. He took a knee to lower his profile and used the breathing room Harris's intervention had created to gun down the remaining cannibals, trusting in Roland's marksmanship.

. . .

Jorge had opted to let Fred drive the old DeSoto as they fled the riverside town of Tow. Leaving wasn't an easy decision, despite how fast he had made it. Jorge knew he was going to get an earful from Roland Reese about not collecting any intelligence on what had happened there, but he also understood that getting Fred out of there would be seen as the priority.

Even though they hadn't hung around to conduct 'man on the street' interviews and dust for fingerprints, all three of them had readily agreed it was a safe assumption the Gen 2 vaccine had turned those who had taken it into the black-eyed cannibals. The obvious question was: Had what happened to everyone at Tow been the exception or the rule?

According to Fred, the entire City State of Houston had gone dark. There were at least a million people there, and they had certainly received the Gen 2 vaccine first. Could there be a million of those things out there? And if there were, in what direction were they headed?

"Where are we going?" Fred asked.

It was a reasonable question. Jorge's only direction had been to, "Get us the hell out of here!"

"We have to go to Cypress Mill."

"Are you *insane*?" Fred asked sharply. "Didn't

you hear what that woman on the recording said? The same thing that happened here must have happened in Cypress Mill!"

"Be that as it may," Jorge persisted, "that's where all of my people were heading. Which means they're either currently in the fight of their lives and they need every swinging dick on deck or it's a giant nothingburger and we need to link up with them."

"I'm not a fighter!" Fred insisted. "I'm not like you!"

Jorge looked at her. "If you weren't a fighter, you wouldn't be talking to me right now. You'd be in the ground with everybody else who rolled over when things got bad. And you sure as shit wouldn't have pulled that .38 back there. I think you've got more fight in you than you know."

In the back seat, Brian coughed into his hand three times.

"You okay?" Jorge asked.

Brian looked down at his hand and saw blood. "I don't know," he said and held up his hand. "I think I'm messed up."

Fred pulled the car over to the side of the road and stopped. She looked at Brian in the rearview mirror and then looked into his eyes.

"*Shit,*" she said under her breath.

Jorge turned around and looked at Brian. "It's gonna be okay," he said.

"No one ever says that when things are gonna be okay," Brian said dubiously.

Brian's eyes were wide, and his pupils had turned black. The black had yet to consume the entire eye like the Gen 2 cannibals back at Tow. For the moment, it just seemed to affect the pupil.

"Let's all get out of the car," Jorge said, "and we'll figure this out."

Then Brian caught his reflection in the rearview mirror. "Shit," he said quietly.

The three got out of the car, and both Jorge and Fred stepped back from Brian.

"I don't understand," Jorge said.

None of them wanted to say it out loud. They didn't want to say what they all knew.

"I'm infected," Brian said. "I don't know how, but somehow it got into me."

Fred turned to Jorge. "Why not you?" she asked. "They were all over you, too, just like him?"

Brian pointed to his shirt, which was covered in blood. "Back in the truck when I was fighting with the girl," Brian said. "This is all her blood. Jorge barely got a drop on him."

Jorge watched Brian's eyes turn another shade of

black. Brian stumbled backward, put his hand to his forehead, and coughed again. This time, he spat blood onto the ground at his feet.

"Damn," Brian said. He straightened up. Tears were welling in his eyes, but they weren't clear.

It was blood.

"I'm *not* going to turn into one of those things," Brian insisted.

"I know," Jorge said. He reached into his cargo pocket and pulled out the small revolver he'd taken from Fred. "I'll do it."

"*No!*" Fred nearly shouted. "There has to be something we can do! He's still himself!"

Jorge looked at her for a moment and then shook his head. "Wait in the car," he said. "We won't be long."

Jorge followed Brian into an open field beside the road. The boy stopped about one hundred feet in and didn't look back. He stared out into the landscape of Central Texas.

"Is there ... anything you want to say?" Jorge asked. "Or anyone you want me to tell something to?"

Jorge wasn't sure what he was supposed to say in

a situation like this. He'd only done something like it once before, and that hadn't ended well.

"I don't know," Brian said. "I guess everyone I cared about is gone now." He hesitated. "I've got a question, though."

"Tell it."

"Did we deserve it?" Brian asked. "All this? Did we have it coming?"

"What do you mean?"

"People. Maybe we screwed things up enough and treated each other bad enough that—"

The gunshot echoed across the field, and Brian's body fell to the ground. Jorge felt the tears welling in his eyes, but he blinked hard and wiped them away. He didn't know why he was getting so emotional; he'd barely known the kid. Still, just like the girl Fred had killed in Tow, Brian hadn't deserved this.

"We didn't have it coming," Jorge said quietly.

Fred watched Jorge walking back out of the field. He pulled open the passenger side door and slid in next to Fred. They were both silent for a moment.

"If it can spread like that ..." Fred ventured. "What are we going to do?"

Jorge said nothing. He just stared out the windshield.

"I guess I always thought there was a chance things could go back to some semblance of normalcy," Fred went on. "At least as long as the City States were able to hold out. I know they weren't perfect, but maybe they could have eventually gotten it right. That's why I stayed in that barn and pretended like none of it was happening. I guess I can't pretend anymore."

Jorge looked down at the gun in his hand and then back out the windshield. "We could finish it here," he said tentatively. "If you want."

"What do you mean?" Fred asked.

Jorge looked at her, and his eyes gave her the answer she had asked for.

"*No*," Fred said firmly. "I want to live. That's what this was always about. Even if I was going about it the wrong way, that's what I want. I don't want to die." She looked out toward the field. "And I sure as hell don't want to die like *that*."

Jorge nodded. "Maybe we just need to say it out loud once in a while," he said. "So we don't forget it."

CHAPTER 4

Cotton walked quickly to the rear of the first truck that had pulled up to the front gate after the shooting had stopped. He lowered the tailgate, pulled an ammo box toward him, and ripped it open.

"You're welcome," Roland said sarcastically as he walked up to his old friend.

"This ain't over," Cotton said as he began topping off his magazines.

"Sure as shit looks over to me," Randall Eisler said as he surveyed the dead bodies littering the ground.

"That's the second wave," Cotton replied, scanning the perimeter as he loaded his AR mags and reseated them in his chest harness. "First wave is still out there."

"And these are different," Harris said. "They're not like the first ones."

Roland turned to Harris, the fire in his eyes impossible to miss. "And what in the hell, exactly are you doing out here?" Roland snapped.

Harris visibly took a step back. It wasn't every day he was chastised by a former member of the world's pre-eminent Tier 1 special operations unit. He thought for a moment about what he should say and decided to go with the truth.

"We came out here to take this town," he said. "And then we figured we'd hit Oatmeal after that."

"Wait a minute," Randall Eisler said. "You're tryin' to tell me you skinned out in the middle of that fight at the farmhouse so you could run behind our backs and take my town?"

"That's about the size of it, yeah," Harris confirmed.

Randall Eisler reached for his sidearm, but Cotton quickly reached out and stayed his hand. "If it weren't for him, I'd be dead," he said reasonably.

"Take your hand off me!" Randall Eisler growled.

Cotton glared at the man. "I'm telling you, he lives," he said firmly. "If you've got an idea to the contrary and you're willing to fall on your sword over it, then I'm willing to make that arrangement."

"Okay," Roland said, stepping between the two. "This ain't happening. We've most likely got enemies on all sides. The last thing we need is to be turning on each other."

Cotton released his grip on Randall Eisler's wrist, and the man returned his pistol to its holster.

"I get it," Cotton said, still talking to Randall Eisler. "Your people are probably all dead. I'm not going to stand here and pretend I wouldn't want to put holes in the first person I saw I could connect to it."

Randall Eisler said nothing.

Cotton turned to Harris. "But I'm betting you know a lot we don't about what the hell went on here."

Harris relayed his story to the men, including his conversation with June Kennedy and locking himself in the big rig to escape becoming lunch.

The part about June hit Randall Eisler hard, but he did his best not to let it show. The last thing he needed was for the others to think he might be romantically involved with a creature that, by

Harris's account, was now leading an army of insane black-eyed cannibals that almost certainly wanted all of them dead.

"So, everyone who got the Gen 2 vaccine went Gen 2 cannibal," Randall Eisler summarized.

"That's about the size of it," Harris replied.

"One thing I don't understand," Roland said as he surveyed the dead bodies littering the ground. "You said, after a while, they all left. Why did June leave these behind?"

"These ones are different," Harris said. "These were slower and weaker. Their skin is paler than the others, too, if that's relevant. Hell, those other ones were like a bunch of overheating engines. They come at you and it's like a rabid dog someone shot up with PCP. These ones ... Hell, I just hit one hard enough with my elbow and it fell over."

Cotton thought about that. He'd gotten lucky. If he'd been faced with the other kind, the cannibals Harris was talking about, there was no way he would have made it out of the town square.

"It's a mutation."

Everyone turned to where Jean Wiley was standing with April, away from the main gathering.

"What's that now?" Roland asked.

"A mutation," Jean repeated. "A variant. The

scientists talked about it with the virus. Remember how as it mutated, it kept getting stronger; picking up speed? They said it wasn't supposed to do that; that it wasn't following the rules. Viruses are supposed to get weaker as they mutate, not stronger."

"That's why a lot of folks thought it was man-made," Randall Eisler confirmed.

"Well, this sounds a lot like that," Jean continued. "Except it's following the rules. It's mutating and spreading, but it gets weaker as it spreads."

"I know I'm new here," April said, "but where did the Gen 2 vaccine come from?"

Roland and Randall Eisler looked at each other.

Roland turned to April. "We got it from Houston."

"So, we can assume they all got it first," April said.

"Guess so," Roland confirmed.

"How many people live in Houston?" Cotton asked.

There was silence for a moment.

Roland broke it. "About a million."

. . .

Cotton turned to the sound of a vehicle coming at them further down the road and brought his weapon up to the low ready.

"Now what?" Roland asked as he stepped into the road.

"I could be wrong," Randall Eisler said as he leaned forward a bit and squinted his eyes, "but I do believe that's a forty-eight DeSoto."

"I know that car," Roland stated.

As the vehicle drew closer, everyone saw that it was indeed a perfectly restored 1948 DeSoto. The car finally pulled to a stop a few dozen feet from the convoy, and Cotton felt his body relax as he identified Jorge in the passenger seat.

"Shit," Roland said. "That's Doctor Fred."

"Who the hell is Doctor Fred?" Cotton asked.

"She does some work for me," Roland replied. "But more importantly, she hasn't stepped outside of Tow for nearly a year. If she's here, she ain't bringin' good news with her."

Cotton saw the look in Jorge's eyes before anyone else did, maybe because he'd seen it so many times in his career. Something had happened to the man, and it had been bad.

"What happened?" Cotton asked.

Jorge looked beyond the group to the bodies

surrounding them. "I'm guessing the same thing that happened here," he said. "These black-eyed cannibals … they overran Tow."

"Any survivors?" Roland asked.

"You're looking at them," Jorge said.

Roland walked to Fred and put his hand on her shoulder. "You okay?"

"I'm fine," Fred replied.

Roland looked into the car and then back to Jorge. "Where's the kid?"

Jorge set his jaw but said nothing.

"It spreads," Fred said. "He didn't make it."

"Is it the vaccine?" Roland asked.

Fred nodded. "And it's not just the vaccine," she said. "It's in the blood. If you get enough of it in a cut or in your mouth or eyes, you turn into one of them. A weaker version, but the outcome's the same."

Sudden realization struck Cotton. "That could be intentional."

"Say what now?" Roland asked.

"Transmission. Increasing the size of the horde by not killing everyone." Cotton pointed to the dead on the ground. "I'm pretty sure they deliberately infected those people and effectively left them behind as an occupying force."

"Shit," Roland spat. "Okay, if that's the case we

can't waste any more time here. We need to get to Oatmeal with a quickness."

"We can't go," Cotton said.

"What do you mean we can't go?"

"Exactly what I said," Cotton replied. "This is where our road ends."

Roland looked at the rest of the group and then stepped closer to Cotton and lowered his voice. "I need you on this," the Master Chief said.

"I get it," Cotton replied. "But I almost bought it running that recon gig through the town for you. I've got too much at stake here and the bottom line is, this isn't my fight. Way I figure it, this Gen 2 thing is only a problem if you're already vaccinated."

"You still ain't figured it out, have you?" Roland asked.

"Figured what out?"

"You're not gonna make it on your own. Not out here." Roland gestured all around them. "And definitely not out *there*. Who the hell knows what's going on across the rest of the country at this point, and you just want to plow through it like a bull in a china shop?"

"All I know is, there might be a million of those things out there," Cotton said. "And all I have to do is not run into them."

"And how are you going to do that, exactly?"

"Same way I've done everything in my life," Cotton said. "A little bit of luck and a lot bit of violence."

"I can't talk you out of this, can I?" Roland asked.

"Sorry," Cotton said. "It's just not my fight." He looked back toward Jean and April. "I have to get her someplace safe."

"What if *this* is the safest place?" Roland continued. "I know it's a bitter pill to swallow, but it might be the truth."

"I can't think that way."

Roland held his old teammate's gaze for a moment and then shook his head. "Take what you need. You can take the vehicle, too, obviously."

"I appreciate that."

"I was never gonna try to mess with you," Roland said. "You know that, right?"

"I know."

"We're leaving?" Jean asked.

"Reckon we are," Cotton said as he began securing the gear in the truck.

The vehicle was already loaded up with a decent amount of emergency supplies, so he didn't imagine they needed to spend more time in Cypress Mill scavenging for anything extra. The less they lingered in Central Texas, the better.

"What's the plan?" April asked. "Where do we go now?"

Cotton thought back to his conversation with Sergeant Major Wikham. Wik was still human. Maybe Cotton should have learned some lesson at this point about how cannibals and humans could work together for the common good or something like that, but he just couldn't let it go. They *ate* people. When everything else was said and done, that one incontrovertible fact remained.

"Might be someone we can link up with out there," Cotton said. "At least get a better idea of the bigger picture and see what we might be dealing with."

"The man in the road," Jean surmised.

Damn, she's sharp, Cotton thought to himself.

He looked around and then lowered his voice. "We need to keep the circle tight on that," he said, and then looked to April. "Understand?"

April nodded.

Cotton closed the door of the 4Runner and watched Roland, Jorge, and Randall Eisler walk toward him. April was driving again, and he rode shotgun while Jean occupied the rear of the vehicle.

Roland rapped the hood twice and smiled. "We're heading to Oatmeal," he said. "Damn near a straight shot, forty-five minutes northeast. You can raise us on the same frequency you've been using if you need to."

"Thanks," Cotton said. "And I do appreciate all you've done, getting me set up and all." He looked past them to where Harris stood in the distance. "What about him?"

Randall Eisler followed his gaze. "Jury's still out," he said. "If he stays useful, maybe he lives."

"He did step up," Cotton pointed out. "At the end there. He could have run, but he didn't."

"We'll take that into consideration," Roland said.

Both Roland and Randall Eisler waved their goodbyes, but Jorge remained.

"Shame we didn't get to know one another better," he offered.

"Maybe it wasn't meant to be," Cotton said with a smile. "Ships passing in the night and all that."

"Be careful out there," Jorge said. "It ain't gettin' any safer."

"That's what everyone keeps telling me."

. . .

Jorge watched Cotton, April, and Jean drive away and could feel something in his gut telling him it was the wrong move. There was the conscious realization that the threats spreading throughout the Texas Meat Belt were only escalating, but there was also something deeper tugging at him.

He felt like he should be going with them.

That, however, was a non-starter. Based on what had happened in Tow and now seeing the condition Cypress Mill was in, it was a reasonable assumption that Oatmeal wasn't much better off. He had to get there and make sure Sheila was safe. He had no illusions that she was going to suddenly turn over a new leaf and melt into his arms, but he felt he owed it to her at least to do what he could to help her.

For the thousandth time, Jorge wondered to himself why the hell he had told her what he did, about how he had killed the President. It had been such a weight for him to bear for so long, and Roland Reese had been the only other person who knew the truth. For some reason, Jorge had thought that sharing his dark secret with Sheila would draw them closer and perhaps smooth out what had been a rocky relationship from the start.

Instead it had done the opposite.

"You okay?" Randall Eisler asked.

Jorge snapped out of his thoughts and turned to the man. "As well as can be expected," he said. "You?"

Randall Eisler shrugged. "Same." He looked back to Cypress Mill, and Jorge could see there was something deeper there. "Guess it hasn't quite hit me yet. That it's all done."

Jorge thought for a moment. "You know, it's none of my business," he ventured, "but I know there was something there. Between you and June."

Randall Eisler smiled. "Was it that obvious?"

Jorge laughed. "You're a slick guy, Randall Eisler. Always have been—but maybe not that slick."

"Yeah," Randall Eisler agreed lazily. "And now it looks like the woman I ... She's the Queen of the Dammed or some shit."

"You know, we don't know much about this Gen 2 yet. Hell, we don't know a *damn thing*. So, we also don't know if it's permanent."

Randall Eisler surveyed the bodies littering the ground. "Looks pretty damn permanent to me. And based on what that son-of-a-bitch Hawthorne said, sounds like she was the leader. Like all the others were the animals or something, but June was still ... herself. Kind of."

Jorge nodded. He wasn't sure what to say. It was

clear that Randall Eisler was having more trouble with this than he was letting on.

"Okay," Roland Reese said to the assembled men. "We're on a war footing. We need to expect heavy fighting and, more importantly, be ready for it. You're all vetted by now. Every single one of you made it through the fight at the farmhouse. I've been through damn near twenty years of war at the highest possible level, and I'll tell you right now, *that* was the worst damn fight I've ever found myself in. I even left a round in my pocket so that when I finally went into slide lock for the last time, I'd have one more for myself."

The men were silent. Everyone had already resupplied and checked their weapons and knew what was coming. The concept that there might be a million black-eyed cannibals roaming the Texas Meat Belt had already made the rounds.

"There's no time for fancy tactics or forward reconnaissance, and there damn sure isn't time to teach all that shit to those of you who don't know it. It's gonna be hey-diddle-diddle right up the middle. We're gonna hit Oatmeal head-on and mow down anything in our path. The creatures we're fixing to run into up there won't be like these ones. They'll be stronger and faster, but they won't have weapons and they won't have tactics. Just keep your cool and make every shot count."

There was a collective murmur of affirmation, but nothing beyond that. The men were tired and Roland knew it. They would show up to Oatmeal running on empty, so he hoped to hell it wouldn't be the fight he was expecting.

Roland walked through the crowd to where Fred was standing beside her DeSoto. He picked up a spare AR that was in the bed of one of the trucks, as well as three magazines. He stopped at the car and ran his hand across the hood.

"Hell of a car," he said with a smile. "I remember when you started working on her. Come a long way."

Fred looked at it and shook her head. "What the hell was I thinking? The world was falling apart around me and I spent my time restoring a car."

"Best way to ride out the end of the world," Roland said. "Might be to distract yourself until it's over."

"Will it be?" Fred asked. "Over someday?"

Roland didn't answer the question. Instead, he held out the AR and magazines to her.

"I don't know how to use that," she said.

"You know, it's not nearly as surprising that you managed to restore a classic car in the middle of the apocalypse as it is that you managed to get this far without using one of these."

"I didn't sign up for this," Fred said. "Back when we struck our deal. I fix things. I don't do … that."

"You do now," Roland said. "*Everybody* does, if they want to make it out alive."

"I've never even held one!" Fred blurted.

Roland shoved the weapon into her hands, and she grabbed it. "There," he said with a smile. "Got that out of the way." He could see the fear in her eyes just holding the rifle. "Look, keep in mind that when this weapon was developed, part of the government's requirement was that an eighteen year-old had to be able to master it and hit a man-sized target from five hundred meters away in a week. You're a grown woman with a PhD in Astromedicine or whatever the hell it is you do, so it shouldn't take nearly as long."

For the next few minutes, he gave a brief lesson on how to shoulder the weapon, manipulate the safety, and swap out a magazine.

"Beauty of these things is, there ain't much to them and there ain't much recoil to speak of. This one has a pretty heavy buffer in it, so you're unlikely to feel anything when you pull the trigger."

"Seems kind of silly now," Fred said.

"What's that?"

"I can fix these, but I've never fired one."

Roland smiled. "Yeah, I always thought that was a little weird."

Sheila stood at the window and watched the black-eyed creatures walk through the streets of Oatmeal. There were more of them now; more than there had been even an hour prior. There was something different about them, though. Just like there had been with Robert.

These ones weren't nearly as fast as the ones she had fought against in the beginning. They also seemed paler and almost sickly. Sheila had seen at least one fall over just walking down the street. It had got back up again, but even then, it appeared unsteady.

She turned and looked around the room again. Was she missing something? For an armory, the room was well stocked with anything a person might need to wage war outside, but it was woefully lacking in anything she might use to force her way out.

With one exception. Sheila walked to the large steel locker on the left and opened it. Inside, she found rolls of detonation cord, blocks of C4 plastic explosive, and ignition switches. Her logic hadn't changed on using it; blowing her way out would almost certainly kill her in the process. It wasn't even that the heat would kill her; it would be the overpressure. The concussive wave from the blast would fill the room, like forcing a gallon of water into a quart size container, and if it didn't actually crush her body, it would liquify her organs.

Sheila recalled there was a way to set up a breaching charge to make the blast go in a certain direction, but she had no idea how to do something like that. As it was, she barely remembered how to set up the det cord and igniter. She only knew that much from standing off to the side while Roland had talked a few men through how to do it.

Then a thought occurred to her: What if there were a hole in the bottom of that quart container for the gallon of water to shoot through? What if there was an exit point in the room for the blast to pass through?

She looked at the window and then back to the door. They were straight across from each other. In theory, if she blew them both at the same time, she wouldn't be crushed by the overpressure filling the room. Effectively, it would just be like standing in the strongest wind tunnel ever built.

In theory.

And this whole scenario created a new problem: if she managed to survive the blast, she would have to be coherent enough to get outside and fight her way through whatever she found.

Sheila turned back to the locker. "Shit," she said quietly. "I'm actually going to do this."

Sheila stopped and surveyed her work. She had lined the window and the doorframe with det cord and placed a single charge at each door hinge. They were as small as she could make them and still imagine they would blow the door off its hinges.

She had cleared out the large steel locker and tested it for its intended purpose. It would work, just barely, but it would work.

Next, she had pulled the best AR-15 she could find, a short barrel Knight's Armament build with a vertical grip installed. The last part was important. Normally, a vertical grip would be set far forward on the lower rail of the rifle to allow the shooter to use it with their non-firing hand and pull the rifle into their shoulder more aggressively to control recoil. Sheila's purpose would be different. She had relocated the vertical grip back to where she could hook her left elbow around it and stabilize the rifle. Seeing as she no longer had a left hand, this was the only way she could reliably fire the AR-15.

If she somehow managed to survive the blast, it was highly unlikely Sheila would simply walk outside and face no opposition. The explosion alone would attract immediate attention, and the black-eyed cannibals were going to be on top of her before she even had time to clear her head.

Sheila pulled the modified AR from the workbench and slid the sling around her body, then tightened it to her body with the pull tab. She looked back out the window and saw that the creatures were still wandering the streets. Granted, they weren't as fast as that first wave, but that damn well didn't mean they were slow.

She held her gaze on the street for a full minute before letting out a breath. She kept harboring fantasies that any moment she would see a truck coming down the street, or Jorge would come running around the corner, but more and more, Sheila was understanding that wasn't going to happen. Whatever was going on in Oatmeal was almost certainly not an isolated event. She couldn't afford to wait around for someone to save her.

No one was coming.

It was time to self-rescue.

Cotton watched Cypress Mill disappear in the rearview mirror as they drove down the main road out of town. It felt good to be in a vehicle again, moving fast. Even if the future was uncertain, at least they were moving again and putting this whole mess behind them.

"Directions?" April asked.

"I was about to ask you the same thing," Cotton replied.

"Still thinking Alaska?"

"There's more to it than what I told you back there. The man in the road was named Wik. He gave me a frequency to contact him on. We might be able to get more information from him to plan our next move."

April seemed to hesitate for a moment. "Do you think he knows a way out?" she asked. "To Alaska?"

"Maybe," Cotton said. "Hard to say. Either way, it can't hurt. Maybe we'll get lucky."

"I wouldn't make it through Canada," April said,

and she looked at Cotton with her milky-white eyes. "They were talking about it while you were out after the fight at the farmhouse. Every other country has a kill order for cannibals."

"A kill order?" Jean asked from the back seat.

"They think we can spread it. Or at least, they don't know we can't. It's assumed most countries have the order in place, but they know for a fact both Canada and Mexico do. Anyone who catches me walking around Canada is most likely to shoot first, ask questions after the fact."

"We'll figure it out," Cotton said. "If we make it that far, we can find a way."

By now, they had traveled a decent stretch down the state road and had begun to pass cars. April pulled the 4Runner off to the side and cut the engine.

"What are you doing?" Cotton asked.

April didn't answer. Instead, she got out and walked alongside the stranded cars until she found what she was looking for. She opened the driver's side door of a small Honda SUV, slid into the driver's seat, turned the key, and started the engine.

"What the hell?" Cotton snapped, jumping out of the 4Runner after her. "I asked what you think you're doing?"

"Making this easy," April said as she stepped out of the car.

"Making *what* easy?"

"This isn't going to work," April said. "Look, whatever it was that happened back at the farmhouse between us ... it just can't work."

"I thought maybe it was a Romeo and Juliet kind of thing," Cotton said with a weak smile.

"They both die at the end."

"I didn't make it that far."

"And Juliet didn't want to eat Romeo's face off."

Cotton laughed.

"You know I'm right," April went on. "There are just too many things that can go wrong. You don't make it trying to drag me along, and I don't make it in the places you want to go."

"So, where does that leave you?"

April looked down the road, back the way they had come. "I'm going to link back up with Roland and Randall at Oatmeal."

"They're your people now?"

April shrugged. "Sometimes your people aren't the ones you would have chosen. They're the ones you find along the way."

Cotton wasn't sure what to say.

April reached out and put her hand on his shoulder. "Watch out for her," she said, nodding toward Jean. "She thinks she can take on the world, but she's still just a little girl."

"You know I will."

April walked around to the back of the 4Runner and opened the tailgate. She pulled out her pack and slung it over her left shoulder, then retrieved her AR. She could feel Jean's eyes on her, and finally she met them.

"You're leaving," Jean said.

"I'm sorry," April replied. "It just doesn't work. You'll be better off without me."

"You don't know that!" Jean snapped.

"You're right," April replied with a nod. "I don't know that, but I have to do what I think is right."

Jean didn't say anything else.

April reached out and put her hand on the girl's shoulder. "Take care of him," April said. "He thinks he can take on the world, but he's still just one man."

Cotton and Jean stood and watched as April pulled the Honda off the hard shoulder and onto the road. Cotton walked to the window and seemed as if he wanted to say something.

"Parting words?" April asked with a smile.

Her smile faded. She could see that something serious was on his mind.

"It's what you said about the kill order for cannibals in other countries."

"What about it?" April asked.

"A while back, I saw Polish mercenaries, when we were traveling through Arkansas."

"Polish?" April asked, her confusion obvious.

"There's been talk for a while about foreign fighters being here, in the United States. That was the only time I saw them with my own eyes, but I did see them."

"Why do you think they're here?"

"It's not outside the realm of possibility that they're here to kill cannibals."

"Why?"

"Clear the way for an invasion force, maybe, or just whittle away at the problem over the next decade. Look, I'm not saying that's one hundred percent what they're doing here, but it makes sense."

"Okay," she said. "I'll be careful."

"There's something else. The Russians will be here soon."

"Who told you that?" April asked. "Wik?"

Cotton nodded.

"When were you going to say something?"

Cotton parted his lips and then paused. "I don't know," he "I think I may have some trust issues."

April smiled. "We'll see each other again, Wiley," she said. "I don't know how I know that, but I do."

"We shouldn't have let her go," Jean said as she and Cotton watched April drive away.

"Weren't gonna be able to stop her," Cotton replied. "Once folks get something in their head, you can't talk them out of it."

"Sounds like someone I know," Jean said.

Cotton looked down at her. "Are we entering the sassy phase?"

"Yeah," Jean replied. "It starts right after the 'cannibal killing' phase. At least, that's what the books say."

Cotton laughed. Yes, she was *definitely* entering the sassy phase.

He pulled the paper he had written Wik's frequency on out of his pocket and showed it to her.

"The man in the road?" Jean asked.

"His name was Wik," Cotton said. "He was in 1/8 after I was, so there's some credibility."

"But we still don't trust anyone," Jean clarified.

"Right," Cotton agreed. "But if he's for real about this safe passage ... he's our best chance at finding a safe route out of here."

"So, what's the next move?"

"Wik said to get a hold of him at dusk or dawn on this frequency, but it's a safe bet that's when he sets up his long range antennae and he was figuring we'd be well out of range by the time we actually got a hold of him."

"Want to give it a try?" Jean asked, nodding to the radio set in the 4Runner.

Cotton walked to the driver's side, leaned in, and keyed in the frequency from the paper into the radio, then picked up the handset.

"This is the SEAL calling for the man in the road," Cotton said.

It wasn't quite strict military protocol, but without established call signs, it was the safest way Cotton could think of to transmit comms without giving anyone away. They waited for a moment in silence until the radio crackled to life.

"That was fast," Wik said from the other end. *"Ready for extraction?"*

"Affirmative," Cotton said.

There was a pause for a moment and then Wik came back. *"Okay, I've triangulated your location, which means anyone else listening in can do the same. Pull your power source and move three clicks south. I'll pop smoke in thirty minutes. Come find me. Color will correlate to who we crush in the game."*

"Roger that."

Cotton hung the handset back on the receiver and immediately reached back and disconnected the power source from the radio.

"'Who we crush in the game?'" Jean asked.

"Army," Cotton said with a smile. "Army vs. Navy football game. He's gonna pop green smoke."

CHAPTER 5

Roland could feel that his nervous system was locked in 'fight or flight' mode. When they had first rolled from Oatmeal for the farmhouse, he hadn't thought much of the trip. It was really just a lark; an excuse to get out of the community. Granted, he'd wanted a firsthand look at what was going on, but he hadn't expected much to come of it. He sure as hell hadn't expected all this.

Now, he was expecting a fight, as were all of the men with him. The battle at the farmhouse had decimated their ranks and made Roland much more aware of just how little in control of Central Texas they actually were. Finding Cypress Mill in the condition they had was another severe blow.

He also couldn't get the idea out of his head that

Oatmeal could be in the same condition. So far, they hadn't been able to raise anyone, either on the radios or on the satellite phones. That wasn't supposed to happen.

If Oatmeal had fallen in the same way Cypress Mill had, that meant they were on their own. In less than twenty-four hours, everything had changed. Not that it mattered much, not if he was being honest about it.

Back in Iraq and Afghanistan, he'd always preferred these kinds of jobs; running lean, more like a rogue out on his own than part of the collective. It wasn't unusual for Roland to take a sniper rifle, a Gatorade bottle full of water and another for spitting, jump on a dirt bike, and just disappear for a few days. No one had ever questioned it because he'd always come back with a string of kills, some confirmed by Marine or Army units he'd run into and some not.

That was a big part of why he'd pushed back so hard against promotion to Master Chief and then even harder against being called up for Command Master Chief. He didn't want it. He wanted to be back on his dirt bike out in the desert, doing what he did best. Maybe that was how it should be again.

He turned to Mitchell, who was driving the Mercedes SUV.

"What's your take?" Roland asked.

Mitchell looked at his Chief for a moment before focusing back on the road. The man wasn't former military, like most of the people Roland trusted the most. Before everything fell apart, Mitchell had led a pretty simple life as a journeyman carpenter. He would swing a hammer for eight hours a day, then go home to his trailer, watch his favorite shows, pass out, and then do the same thing the next day. He liked it that way, favoring the predictability of it. He'd never considered himself a prepper or harbored any fantasies of being in the military. As a matter-of-fact, the only firearm he owned was an old Colt revolver handed down from his father and his father before him.

As a result, Mitchell wasn't a fan of the new world and its inherent unpredictability. Still, he did his part to keep things going in what he perceived to be the right direction, and a big part of that was working for Roland.

"My take?" Mitchell asked.

"This whole thing. Which direction you think it's going?"

"You mean the Cannibal Queen?"

Roland laughed. "Is that we're calling her now?"

"Didn't take the guys long to come up with that," Mitchell said with a smile, then he became more serious. "You want my unvarnished opinion?"

"Wouldn't ask if I didn't," Roland replied.

"Way I see it, we need to—"

Roland felt the splatter across his face and heard the cracking of glass, but unlike a normal person, it took him no time at all to process what had happened. In that split second, he jerked the steering wheel to the left, taking them off the road and into an embankment, where the vehicle hit a grassy berm.

Someone had shot Mitchell through the windshield.

Roland threw himself out of the passenger side door and took cover with his AR behind the engine block as a volley of rounds shredded the SUV. He could see the other vehicles in the convoy trying to take evasive maneuvers, but they weren't having any more luck than he was. They were being slaughtered.

Then he saw it: the glint of a scope on a nearby overpass.

"You done fucked up now!" Roland snarled. "You picked a gunfight with the wrong sniper!"

There was a brief lull in the firing, no doubt as

the opposition force were reloading, and Roland took this opportunity to scamper up the side of the berm with his AR. A few rounds hit the ground around him, but none were close to making contact. Once over the top, he hit the dirt and popped the covers off the Leupold scope. He knew he wasn't going to have the kind of range with his 12.5 inch barrel that he would have had with a full length recce rifle like Jorge's, but it would get the job done either way.

Roland reached down and keyed the radio on his vest. "J-12, this is Chieftain. You breathing?"

There was a pause for a moment and then Jorge's voice came back. *"Roger that. Ready to make contact."*

"Send them to hell."

Roland crawled to the edge of the embankment and popped his head over the top, just enough to pick up the glint on the overpass again. Whoever this guy was, he didn't seem to understand that his scope reflected light.

The range was about three hundred meters out, and judging by the feel of it against the side of Roland's face, the wind was only about five miles per hour. In one smooth movement, he slid his rifle over the embankment, brought his eye to the scope, found his hold on the reticle, and broke the wall on the trigger.

The glint on the overpass made a fast, jerking motion. He'd hit his target.

Further down the road, Roland heard another series of shots, but this time, he could tell that it was a gunfight, not just whoever the hell these guys were taking shots at them from a distance.

No time for finesse, Roland ran over the embankment and down to the pavement again. There were enough abandoned cars on the road that if he could just make it down the slope without getting his head turned into a canoe, he'd have a fighting chance.

Jorge kept his foot nailed to the ground and his eyes on the offset red dot on his recce rifle. He lay in what they had come to call "urban prone" and watched the boots walking by on the other side of the truck he was taking cover behind. Urban prone was much like the prone position he had first learned in the military, except that instead of being on your belly on the ground, you lay more on your side. It was a more realistic firing position and caused shooters to be less banged-up in the long term, as hitting the ground in the traditional prone over and over again took a toll on a man's body through the years.

Who the hell are these guys? Jorge thought to himself as he watched a half dozen of them casually walking through the street.

They were all wearing military uniforms, and unlike a lot of the survivors running around the Texas Meat Belt, these were organized, with unit patches and everything. This was an actual military force, but they weren't American. If Jorge remembered his unit insignia correctly, they were Polish.

It was obvious the Poles thought they were ambushing a bunch of yokels driving through Central Texas, but they had picked the wrong convoy. Roland had already sent that message to the sniper on the overpass, but apparently these guys hadn't gotten the memo and needed an extra reminder.

It was a calculated risk. Jorge had no idea how many more of these men there might be on the road, but he also knew he couldn't afford to let them walk by and possibly get flanked.

He flicked off the safety on his recce rifle and pulled the trigger at a fast rhythm, ten total shots into the men walking by, more specifically into their legs. Men who can't stand are going to be bad at fighting.

From there, Jorge rolled into a deep squat and stood up, button-hooking around the rear of the truck and angling his offset red dot to begin picking up targets. He'd always thought the offset red dots were a little gimmicky and preferred mounting his on top of the scope or not having one at all. Now, it made more sense; it allowed him to angle around the corner of the truck without exposing too much of his body. It was like shooting fish in a barrel.

A few of the Poles were trying to get their weapons up, but Jorge put rounds through each in turn. He then moved from cover to the last man and dropped to a kneeling position, landing the knee in question directly on the man's neck.

"Who are you?" Jorge snapped as he looked around and changed out the magazines in his AR.

He was out in the open. It was a bad position and he knew it, but he also knew that he might not get another opportunity to interrogate one of the opposing force.

The man began muttering something in Polish.

Jorge responding by pushing his suppressor into the man's arm, which was met with a scream. The YHM Turbo T2 suppressor could reach thirteen hundred degrees, and that amount of heat meeting human flesh was a strong persuasion tool.

"*Talk!*" Jorge shouted as he held the suppressor over the man's face.

"United Nations!" the man cried out and then continued to speak in broken English. "We are here on a United Nations mission!"

"What the hell are you talking about?"

"We were deployed to clean up!"

Jorge felt the world drop out from beneath him. "'Clean up?'" he asked. "You mean, kill cannibals?"

The man said nothing.

Jorge felt a round snap past his head and launched himself forward without thinking. He scrambled up the embankment to a car dealership perched on the side of the road. A series of rounds impacted all around him as he sprinted through the open lot toward the main office. There was no time to stop and assess; he needed to find some more significant cover.

The windows of the dealership had all been smashed long ago, so it was easy enough for Jorge to run through one of the open windows and enter the building. He felt something hit his left side but didn't give it much thought until he was down a hallway and through a door that led into the service area.

Jorge took a knee and checked his shoulder. It was a flesh wound, but he grabbed his blow out kit and quickly dressed it with a bandage. Next, he retrieved his radio and hit the call button. "Chieftain, this is J-12. You out there?"

"*Affirmative,*" Roland replied. "*Engaging targets of opportunity—and there's a freakin' lot of 'em.*"

Jorge looked down the hallway and could hear bullets peppering the internal walls.

"Think I know how to take 'em," Jorge said. "You know where I am?"

Despite the fact that Jorge and Roland's radios were encrypted, they still maintained some semblance of radio discipline. If they were really going up against a legit UN force, it was only a matter of time before the Poles broke their encryption.

"*Affirmative,*" Roland replied. "*I'll meet you in three.*"

"One more thing," Jorge said. "They're U.N."

There was a pause for a moment.

"*What the hell did you just say?*" Roland asked, sure he must have heard wrong.

"You heard me," Jorge said. "Come around the back. I'll let you in."

. . .

Jorge held his position at the rear of the service bay and watched the rear parking lot through the narrow window until he saw Roland running toward him. He could hear the shots and see the small fragments of cement ricocheting around the SEAL Master Chief.

"Damn," Jorge said to himself as he watched Roland. "There were a hundred other ways you could have done that."

Once Roland was within a dozen feet of the door, Jorge opened it and the man ran in. Jorge slammed the door shut.

Roland immediately dropped to one knee and threw up.

"I guess you ain't been hittin' the Peloton lately," Jorge said with a smile.

"My cardio has suffered in the apocalypse," Roland replied. He stood back up and checked his rifle and gear. "What's the plan?"

"They're playing our game now."

Randall Eisler flattened himself as best he could against the truck bed as rounds flew overhead and shattered the rear windshield. He'd been driving with a couple of his guys and that son-of-a-bitch Hawthorne when the convoy had been ambushed.

Now, he was alone. He'd tried to exit into the street but had immediately felt as if the entire state of Texas was shooting at him. He hadn't experienced this volume of gunfire since Iraq, and he'd hoped never to run into it again.

Without giving much thought to the maneuver, Randall Eisler had scrambled up into the bed of the truck to take what little cover it afforded. There were so many rounds flying and pinging off the body of the truck that it was actually rocking from side to side.

"Well," he said to himself as he lay flat on his back. "We had a good run."

Absurdly, in that moment, he looked up to the blue sky and thought about how beautiful it was. Maybe if it all had to end, this was as good a way as any.

Then he heard the squealing of tires and felt something slam into the rear of the truck.

"Get in!"

Randall Eisler threw out his foot and kicked loose the tailgate of the truck. "I'll be a son-of-a-bitch," he said with a smile.

Harris Hawthorne looked back at him from the front seat of a battered Ford Expedition.

With no more hesitation, Randall Eisler crawled across the truck bed and into the back of the SUV, then closed the tailgate. Every window in the vehicle was being shot out, but Harris just sat there waiting, as calmly as if he were on his way to an ice cream social.

Once Randall Eisler had closed the tailgate, Harris floored it and pulled a one-eighty in the middle of the road.

"Where is everyone?" Randall Eisler shouted.

"Dead!" Harris replied, and he accelerated up the side of the embankment toward the car dealership.

Jorge held position on one side of the service bay while Roland staked out the other, both men at opposing angles to the door the Polish troops were most likely to enter through.

"What the fuck is the U.N. doing here?" Roland snarled as they waited.

"Cannibal cleanup," Jorge replied.

"Makes sense in a weird way," Roland responded. "The Russians and the Chinese were both pretty much running the United Nations before this whole mess started. No reason I can see that would have changed."

"And these guys are clearing the way for an invasion force."

Roland nodded.

The sound of glass crunching underfoot carried down the hallway, followed by voices heading their way.

"Let them in," Roland said and then caught himself. "Shit, you know what to do."

Jorge smiled.

The door to the service bay swung inward and the Polish soldiers piled in, moving toward the center of the bay. The idea was to let the opposing force fill up the room and cluster themselves in the center before sending them the good news.

Jorge held up three fingers and dropped them one at a time. When the final finger had dropped, he leaned out from his crouched position and began taking slow, well-aimed shots at the men who had entered the room. Roland did the same, with predictable results.

It was mass chaos. The Polish troops tried to

counterattack, but the combination of Jorge and Roland's suppressors and the concrete walls of the room made it impossible for them to pinpoint the two men's positions.

Along the left side of the room, Jorge watched some of the men turn and run back through the door, out into the hallway they had come from.

"I don't think so!" Jorge snapped, and he sprinted forward with his rifle up, laying down steady fire as he crossed the room and entered the hallway.

There were bodies everywhere as he moved through the hall and back into the main room of the dealership. As he emerged, he saw a dozen men gathered in the center of the room with their weapons up. Jorge performed a speed reload of his rifle and began firing into the cluster, but he only got two rounds off before his bolt locked back.

Without thinking, he slapped the bottom of the magazine and racked the charging handle, then pulled the trigger. Nothing.

"Shit," he said quietly. He was out in the open. There was no cover, and his Colt was still in its holster, velcroed below the steering wheel of his truck.

Jorge saw it before the Polish troops did. He turned to the left and watched the Ford Expedition speeding across the parking lot toward one of the few intact windows, whereupon the SUV slammed through it and plowed into the assembled group of soldiers.

Jorge used the distraction to find cover behind the reception desk and get his rifle back in the game. No sooner had he cleared the malfunction than he heard the steady *pop* of AR-15s. He leaned back out from behind the desk and saw Hawthorne and Eisler executing what remained of the Polish troops at point blank range.

"*Friendly!*" Jorge shouted before standing up.

Randall Eisler smiled. "Good to see we weren't the only ones to make it out of that shit show alive."

Jorge walked to the Expedition, looked around, and then focused on Harris. "You did this?" he asked.

"Yes, sir," Harris replied. He knew very well he was talking to a real life member of Delta Force, the United States Army's premier Special Missions Unit. The very thing he had always dreamed of being a part of.

"Balls of steel, man," Jorge said with a smile.

The door to the service bay opened and Roland Reese walked out. "What in hell happened out here?" the Master Chief hollered.

"Super Soldier here saved the day," Randall Eisler said, indicating Harris.

"No shit?" Roland asked.

"Just trying to do my part," Harris replied modestly.

Roland looked around. "Are we seriously all that's left?"

"Near as I can tell," Jorge said.

"Wait a minute," Roland said. "Where's Fred?"

Jorge ran down the embankment toward the upturned DeSoto on the side of the road. By the looks of it, the vehicle had been hit by some kind of explosive. He'd thought he'd seen or heard a couple of RPGs zipping around during the initial ambush, and by the looks of things, the classic car had taken one right up the tailpipe.

The rest of the men came down after him.

"Fan out!" Roland ordered. "Find her!"

April slowed the Honda SUV and leaned forward to get a better look at the road ahead of her. She didn't see anything, so she brought the vehicle to a stop and cut the engine. She listened.

There it was again: the steady *pop, pop, pop* of gunfire.

April was no expert, but it sounded like the ARs Roland and his men had been using. Not only that, but it was *a lot* of them.

She started the engine back up again and reversed the vehicle. Whatever the hell was going on ahead of her, it wasn't her fight.

She had just hit the last intersection and was getting ready to turn and head back the way she had come when she saw the truck barreling toward her. April tried to throw the vehicle back into forward drive and get away, but her movements were confused and, instead, the vehicle switched into neutral and the engine quickly stalled.

The truck was coming fast now, so April did the only thing she could think of. She hopped into the back of the SUV, grabbed her rifle, and dropped to the floor.

It felt as if she was trapped inside a steel tornado as the vehicle flipped end-over-end. April felt something crack in her leg and she knew her head was bouncing against something hard, but it was impossible to make any sense of it. She knew only one thing: she was not going to give up her grip on the rifle, no matter what.

Finally, the Honda slid to a stop on its side, having finally landed from the violent impact and skidded across the road. Then it was quiet, to an almost surreal degree. Then the voices. They were speaking a language she didn't know, but it sounded Eastern European—or Russian, maybe. Whatever it was, she knew the men speaking it weren't locals.

"Come out!" a man shouted in heavily accented English. "Cannibal! Come out!"

Well, April thought to herself, *that's not good.*

Moving as slowly as possible, she adjusted her angle in the vehicle and brought the rifle into her side. The footsteps were getting closer.

"Cannibal! Come out!" the man called again.

Come and get me, April thought. *Just a little closer.*

She thought back to the night she had met Cotton and Jean, then realized it had only been a couple of days ago. How had so much happened so fast? That night, she had been ready to kill herself. And for what? *Nothing.* No, that wasn't right. It was *fear* that had driven her to it. She was ready to die out of pure fear.

Now was different. She was ready to die again, but this time, it would mean something. She would die fighting, not like a coward.

Something hit the side of the vehicle and then came through the window above her, hitting the ground beside her. A split second later, it began spewing some kind of gas, and April began coughing violently. Tear gas.

She crawled up through the broken window of the SUV as it lay on its side and emerged with her weapon up, desperately trying to find a target through her red dot.

Then everything went black.

Cotton slowed the 4Runner and found the mile marker he was looking for. Once he identified it, he sped back up and took the first off-ramp, leading him away from the Interstate and further out into the rural landscape of Central Texas.

"We're there?" Jean asked from the passenger seat.

"About to be," Cotton affirmed.

He continued driving for another mile before pulling off the state road and parking beneath some trees. It could have been a faster trip, but he had decided to take the long way around, partially to draw out anyone who might have been following them. That was the logic behind getting on the Interstate versus sticking to surface roads. It would be much harder for a tail to stay hidden on I-35.

The two stepped out of the vehicle and stood beneath the shade of the oak tree. It wasn't nearly as hot as it had been the day prior, but all the same, they welcomed the cover.

Cotton opened up the back of the truck and retrieved his rucksack, from which he pulled the old pair of binoculars he carried. He popped the lens covers off and brought them to his eyes, scanning the horizon. He wasn't looking for Wik's green smoke; he was again on the lookout for anyone who might be following them.

"There it is!" Jean said excitedly.

Cotton lowered the binos and turned to look in the direction she was pointing. He couldn't help but smile. This was the first time he'd felt like there was a real possibility of making it through this mess. Granted, nothing would ever be "normal" again, but he would settle for not living in constant danger.

"Okay," he said as he shouldered the pack and did a quick once-over of the vehicle, looking for anything he might need. "This is it. We're probably not coming back, so make sure you have everything."

"Already done!" Jean said with a smile. She had her pack on and was holding her MK18.

"Look," Cotton said, "it's important for you to know this might not turn into anything."

"I know," Jean said. "I get it, but it's the only shot we've got."

Cotton nodded. He wanted to say something more to avoid his daughter being crushed if it turned out to be nothing, but he also understood that she was a lot closer to being an adult than she was to being a child.

"Okay," Cotton said. "It's not far, just over that hill, but we need to go back to good patrolling, like we were doing in Arkansas. Remember, we're not home yet."

"Roger that," Jean said and brought her rifle to the low ready.

The two moved forward, keeping as close as possible to the cover of the trees as they headed for the medium-sized hill Cotton had indicated. He had no reason to think they were being followed by anyone, but he still couldn't shake the idea that they were being watched.

They moved up the hill and paused at the top. Cotton knew very well that standing on the top of a hill was a good way to get yourself shot, but there was no way around it, so they crested the apex and looked down into the valley below.

Sure enough, a pickup truck was parked there, and Wik stood beside it.

Cotton felt a wave of relief wash over him. At least they had gotten this far. It didn't mean they were home free, but at least they had made it to the first step.

Cotton and Jean dropped their packs beside the truck and Cotton stepped forward, reaching out to shake Wik's hand.

"Glad you made it," Wik said as he shook Cotton's hand. "Had second thoughts?"

"We need to be with people," Cotton said. "But our goal isn't to get into a fight. I'm just planning to get as far north with you as I can and then break off, if that's all right with you?"

"Understandable," Wik said. "If I was in your position, I'd do the same."

As Jean watched the exchange, she also listened to the radio array in Wik's truck going crazy. "Sounds like a fight," she said as she listened to the shouting interspersed with gunfire.

"Yeah," Wik said. "Sounds like the Poles ran into some trouble they weren't expecting."

"Poles?" Jean asked.

Cotton turned to his daughter. "U.N. forces are out there," Cotton said slowly. "Hunting cannibals."

"What?" Jean asked, her face a mix of surprise and anger. "How long have you known about this?"

"Wik told me back on the road when he stopped us," Cotton said, sensing he might have made a mistake in not telling her.

"They were our friends," Jean said. "They helped us."

"They might have helped us," Cotton said, "but they weren't our friends."

"What about April?"

"That was different," Cotton insisted.

"And Roland?" Jean asked. "He wasn't your friend?"

"We're not having this conversation!" Cotton snapped. "It's over. We have to move on."

"We might have to move on, but this ain't *over*."

"There's something else," Wik said, looking uncomfortable. "They might have gotten their asses kicked down the road a piece by your friends, but they took a woman before the shooting stopped."

"Took her?" Cotton asked.

"I just know what I heard on the radio. One of our guys speaks a little Polish and was able to translate. They snatched some woman in a Honda SUV, out on her own."

"April!" Jean cried.

"What happened to her?" Cotton asked.

"Nothing," Wik said. "Yet. Look, you know how this works. They'll extract whatever intel they can from her and then they'll ..."

"They're going to kill her!" Jean exclaimed.

Cotton looked to his daughter and then back to Wik. "When do we leave?" he asked.

"We ain't *leaving!*" Jean insisted. "We have to help her."

"Negative," Cotton said curtly. "All her cannibal buddies are still out there. They'll find her. We have to get moving."

"You're just going to leave her?" Jean asked in disbelief.

"Yes," Cotton said as he picked up his pack.

"They're going to torture her," Jean said. "And then they're going to kill her!"

"I understand that."

Jean's eyes were welling with tears. "Just like they did to Mom."

It felt like he'd been hit by a big rig. Wik took a step back, sensing that he was in the middle of something he shouldn't be.

"How do you—"

"I found the after action report," Jean said, more quietly. "In your desk. I know what happened. I know *everything*."

Cotton didn't know what to say. She had been so young when it happened, when her mother had been run down by Taliban fighters in Afghanistan. Back then, it had been impossible to tell Jean the truth. As she grew older, somehow it became even more difficult, until Cotton finally decided to just put it away forever.

"It's not the same thing," Cotton said.

"It's *exactly* the same thing," Jean replied. "And you know it."

"I'm sorry, Baby Bear," Cotton said. "I'm sorry you found that and I'm sorry this is happening, but I can't risk our future to go after her. For all we know, she's already dead."

"What's my life worth, then?" Jean returned. "What will it even mean? Is the purpose of my life to run away? To turn my back on the people that mean something to me at the first sign of trouble? To just run forever and hope the bad things never catch up with me? I'm not gonna do it. I'm not that person. *You* didn't raise me that way."

It was just like the other night at the farmhouse,

when she'd refused to leave everyone behind despite the fact that returning to the fight meant almost certain death. Cotton thought about his connection to Roland, a man he had fought and bled beside for nearly twenty years. The warning he had given April was true—he had never one hundred percent trusted Roland—but there was another piece to that puzzle. When it came to a fight, Cotton trusted him all the way, and there was a difference. Yes, he wouldn't leave his dog with the man for the weekend, but if he needed someone to cover him while advancing on an objective, he'd pick Roland Reese every time.

Despite only having known Jorge for a very short time, Cotton also trusted him, and what the man had said back on that hill was true. Jorge had stuck his neck out to help Cotton save his daughter from Barnabas and the Nephilim. No questions asked, he had just plunged forward with him into the darkness.

Perhaps Cotton had become so single-minded in his quest to get his daughter out of the Texas Meat Belt that he had lost sight of his own principles.

"*Shit*," Cotton said. "You're right. We have to go get her."

"I can't wait for you," Wik said. "Sorry, I don't mean to sound like a prick, but it's true. We've got a time hack to link up with some other groups in the north. I was pushing it just to meet you here."

"I understand," Cotton said.

"There's a Toyota dealership in Marble Falls on 281. There was a gunfight there about fifteen minutes ago. Looks like a U.N. ambush. It was probably those folks you were in the convoy with. My guess is, your friend was snatched around there. Our scouts think the Poles are holed up in a rail yard about three clicks due east of that location. No guarantees, but I'd bet money on you finding someone there who can lead you to her."

"Roger that."

Wik looked at Cotton for a moment and then walked back to his truck, reached into a side pocket, and retrieved a ziplock bag with a folded map in it. He reached out and handed it to Cotton.

Cotton took it.

"That can't fall into the wrong hands," Wik warned. "If you get my drift."

"What is it?"

"Freedom Corridor route," Wik replied.

"Freedom Corridor?"

"I wasn't going to say anything about it until I knew more about you. It might not even still be operational, but it was a path through Canada into

Alaska, to a place where people could be left alone."

"This is confirmed?"

"Like I said, its questionable if it's still free and clear, but if it is, it's a way out. There's no guarantee you'll make it, but at least with that map, you've got a chance."

"Thank you," Cotton said, looking at the map. "But what about you? Do you think *you* have a chance?"

"Probably not," Wik said. "But every story needs a good ending. Maybe for America, we're about to write that ending."

Cotton's eyes fixed on the map of the Freedom Corridor, but it took a moment for his brain to process what he was seeing. He looked back to Wik.

"Why does this start in Oklahoma?" Cotton asked. "Why are there red lines everywhere else?"

Cotton knew the answer to his own question, but he needed to hear Wik say it.

The man's eyes were wide. "Shit," Wik said. "I don't know why, but I thought you knew."

"Knew what?" Jean asked.

"The Russians ... they're already here," Wik said. "They've been here for weeks. They've already taken everything north of Texas."

INTERLUDE ONE

June Kennedy stood in the cool shade of the tree cover and looked down at her bare feet. They looked *alive*, for lack of a better word. Every nerve ending was electric, and she felt as if she could actually feel the roots in the soil growing beneath her.

Increasingly, she understood that her entire life up until this point had simply been a prelude. This was real life. *This* was the life she had always been meant for. Everything that had come before was only a ghost of her true potential.

She surveyed the whirling mass of black-eyed cannibals that circled her. They almost seemed to be in orbit around her; the sun that gave direction to their world. Not a God or a Goddess; those were both childish concepts that catered to the human need for clear, sentient direction. The need to validate their existence.

No, she was the sun. She was the life force. Perhaps that was it. The horde were not many different beings; they were one being, one consciousness. One tree with many branches.

June lay down in the leaves that covered the ground and looked up to the sky beyond the canopy. She closed her eyes and could still see them within her consciousness. Her subservients continued to swirl around her; the eye to their hurricane, the life-giving center of their existence.

There was something else, though. On the very edge, bleeding into the periphery like a figure drawn in wet ink and then smeared by the artist's hand, was a phantom. It seemed like it might be a woman. A woman with one arm.

Who are you? June thought.

There was no answer. She waited a moment longer and then put it out of her mind. Whoever this phantom was, she was not part of The Plan.

June sat upright and looked to the west, where a tall hill stood. She rose and walked across the crackling leaves that coated the ground. The horde of black-eyed cannibals parted to make a path for her and then, one by one, filed in behind her until she was leading what seemed like an endless train of them up the tall hill.

For a moment, she became obsessed with her breath; with the feeling of the warm air coating her lungs. Like everything else, it was an entirely new sensation, and she felt as if she could become lost in that sensation alone for all time and never become weary of it.

Finally, she crested the top of the hill. She looked over her shoulder and saw the scores of black-eyed cannibals behind her. She smiled and turned to the valley below, where thousands had gathered to await the center of their universe.

CHAPTER 6

Sheila froze in the darkness of the steel locker.

The words had been very clear, just as clear as the voice she'd heard when she first awoke after entering the armory.

"*Who are you?*" the voice had asked.

Sheila remained silent. She didn't know if this voice would be able to hear her response, and she didn't think it would be wise to draw undue attention to herself at this exact moment in time.

With no little amount of effort, she had been able to latch the door to the storage locker from the inside and keep the piece of wire she had used locked in place so that she could get back out again. The AR with the modified grip was slung tight to her body, and in her right hand, she held the trigger for the breaching charges she had rigged up.

"Okay, God," she said. "Obviously I don't have much experience praying because I'm pretty sure that's not how you start, but if you're in the market for lost souls to lend a hand to, I'm putting out the call. I can't say I'm going to change much or start doing volunteer work, but I'll aim to cut back a bit on the cussing and maybe some of the other stuff, too."

She let out a breath and hit the detonator.

The moment Sheila hit the button, it occurred to her that she should have put on some of the hearing protection from the safety box, but a moment later, she realized it wouldn't have done any good. She could feel the locker crumpling around her as the air was briefly sucked out of the armory and then replaced with the blast. Then the locker spun around, flipped, and landed hard on the other side of the room.

Sheila felt the shockwave hit her and even thought she could feel her internal organs being rearranged, but once it was over, she at least knew she was alive.

"*Holy shit!*" she declared, and then remembered the promise she'd just made. "Sorry, Lord. I said I'd cut back. I didn't say I'd stop."

Sheila dropped the detonator from the death grip of her right hand and grabbed the wire connected to the lock. She yanked it hard and then kicked the doors open. There had always been a possibility the locker would fall facedown on its doors, which would have escalated her situation from bad to horrible, but luckily for her, it had landed on its side, and Sheila unceremoniously spilled out onto the concrete floor. She landed hard on top of the AR, which rewarded her efforts by racking her in the chin with the stock.

"Shit!"

Sheila could taste blood in her mouth as she staggered to her feet and looked around. "*Wow*," she said as she surveyed the damage. "I guess that worked."

Despite having aimed to simply blow out the door and the window, she had damn nearly leveled the building. Two of the four walls were completely gone, part of the roof had fallen in, and the hallway she had entered through was gutted. If the locker had not been constructed from steel, there was no way she would have survived.

Sheila stood up and then quickly steadied herself against what remained of one of the walls. Her balance was still disrupted, and she was gradually becoming aware of the intensity of the ringing in both ears. She pulled the tab to loosen the sling on the AR with her right hand and clamped her left elbow around the vertical fore-grip.

Just in time.

Her peripheral vision registered the threat before her conscious mind did and she brought the AR up, her thumb flicking off the safety, and fired a controlled pair into the black-eyed cannibal charging through the destroyed hallway toward her. Three more were directly behind it, and she braced her back against the wall as she unleashed a torrent of 5.56 rounds into the hallway, cutting them down one by one.

There was no time for strategy; no opportunity to grab anything else. She had stuffed four loaded AR mags into her pockets before climbing into the locker, and for the moment at least, that appeared to be all she would need. Sheila scooped up the small pack she had also loaded up and threw it over her shoulder.

Toward the end of the hallway, she could hear noise, and she saw some commotion as more of the black-eyed cannibals tried to make their way past a section of fallen ceiling. Sheila turned to where the window had been and decided it was the best play to move out into the street. The street wasn't much better, but at least she could get some distance between herself and the cannibal horde.

She stood in the street and watched as the creatures moved through the town. There were so many of them. Was it dozens or scores? A *hundred*?

The numbers didn't mater. What mattered was getting the hell out of there, or at least finding somewhere more secure and with some food, where she could hole up until either someone came or these things decided to move on to greener pastures.

Fred could feel the adrenaline surging through her body as every muscle tensed against the zip ties that bound her wrists and ankles. Nothing highlights a person's lack of flexibility like being hogtied in the back of a truck.

She was quite certain that the binding job the soldiers had done on her had torn her left rotator cuff, but there was no one to complain to about it once they'd covered her mouth with duct tape.

Thus far, all Fred had been able to see was the side of the truck bed she was lying in. She had tried to roll herself over to be able to at least see what points of interest they were passing, so that she could re-trace her route if she somehow managed to escape, even though she had no idea how that would happen.

Instead, she kept a steady count as they drove. If she learned nothing else, she would at least know how long it had taken to get to their destination from the ambush point traveling at a moderate speed. To tell the truth, she really wasn't sure how that was supposed to help her, either, but she thought she'd read a Tom Clancy book a while back where one of the characters did the same thing.

The reality of it was, Fred suspected her time had finally run out. It was bound to happen eventually. Fred had always known she was living in a bit of a dream world thinking that the collapse of civilization was never going to catch up to her. It figured that the day she finally stepped out of her barn and left Tow would be the day she would be abducted and murdered, probably with some torture in between.

In the midst of all this, she had a bizarre thought: she only wished she'd had a chance to fight back. It had all happened too fast. She'd heard shots being fired, and the next thing she knew, she was upside down, the DeSoto flipping end-over-end across the road. Then she was out, and when she came to, she had already been hogtied and was being thrown in the back of the truck.

Resistance was a strange concept to her because she wasn't a fighter, and she never had been. Sure, when she was younger, she'd been able to defend a thesis with the best of them, and during her time at A&M, she'd never hesitated to take the Dean to task over things that were important to her. However, she understood that arguing was not the same as fighting. Up until recently, she had never so much as thrown a punch in her life in anger—or fired a weapon.

Now, that had all changed. Now, that was all she wanted to do. All she wanted was one shot, even if it would mean certain death. She just wanted a fighting chance. Lying in the back of that truck, as defenseless as a human being can possibly be, Fred swore to herself that if she managed to get her hands free, she was going to go out swinging, not like some lamb. She would become the lioness.

After several minutes, the truck finally slowed down and pulled to a stop. She overheard some faint talking and was finally able to put her finger on what language it was. They were speaking Polish.

What the hell are the Polish doing here?

Then another man spoke up, but his language was different, and a couple of the men switched over to this language to converse with him. After a few beats, she realized what it was.

Russian. The Russians are here.

The tailgate dropped open with a loud *clank*, and Fred felt herself being dragged out and unceremoniously dropped to the pavement. The men responsible clipped the zip ties holding her ankles together and stood her up.

She came face to face with a man who appeared to be about her age, maybe early fifties at the most. He wore a United Nations armband but was clearly Russian, and he had gold stars on his epaulets.

"Don't worry," the man said in perfect English. "You're not going to die. We know who you are."

He jerked his thumb toward a line of railcars, and the two soldiers holding Fred by her arms began dragging her toward it.

Trying to be inconspicuous, she looked around and realized where she was. She also noticed that there were crews of men working on rail engines in the yard.

They're going to use the train network, she thought to herself. *Whatever they're here to do, that's how they're going to do it.*

It made sense. If this was the beginning of an invasion, using the country's railway system to move troops around and transport materiel would be the way to do it. There was no air power to stop them; no drones in the sky. The occupying forces could go wherever they wanted and move tons of vehicles, weapons, and supplies with next to no effort.

The two men dragged Fred through a patch of gravel to a waiting railcar, where a third man pulled the door open. Then she felt the needle in her arm. It only took a moment for her to feel as if she were about to pass out, but she didn't quite get that far. They had only sedated her.

The men cut the zip ties binding her hands and pushed her up into the railcar.

Fred wanted to hold true to the vow she had made to herself about wanting to fight back, but her arms and legs felt like concrete and she could barely keep her eyes open. Instead, all she could do was watch as they rolled the door shut and locked it.

She slowly pulled the tape from her mouth and waited a moment while her eyes adjusted to the light.

"I know you," she heard a voice say in the semi-darkness.

After another moment, Fred's eyes adjusted enough for her to make out the face on the other side of the railcar.

"From Cypress Mill," Fred said.

It was April.

"We didn't meet," April said. "I'm April. I was with Cotton."

"I remember him," Fred said. "I think we might be in trouble."

"I figured that one out for myself."

"No, I mean *real* trouble," Fred said. "They said they know who I am."

"You worked for Roland," April said. "Fixing things, right?"

"I did, but a long time ago, I used to do other things. Specifically, for the United States Government."

"Like what?"

"Damn it," Fred said, obviously angry with herself. "I should have been more careful. I just never thought in a million years something like this could happen."

"Something like *what?*" April asked, more insistently. "What did you do for the government?"

Fred hesitated for a moment before answering. "I designed the base level encryption for the nuclear ballistic missile program."

April whistled. "Does that mean what I think it does?"

"It means anyone who gets inside my head could potentially control the entire nuclear arsenal of the United States of America."

"That sounds bad," April said flatly.

"It is bad. About as bad as it gets."

"As bad as this?" April asked, pointing to her leg.

Fred's eyes were immediately drawn to a piece of April's shinbone poking through the skin.

"*Holy shit!*" Fred screamed.

"Keep your voice down!" April snapped.

"Your bone! It's sticking through your skin!"

"*I know!*" April responded. "But seeing as how I'm the one with my freaking bone sticking out of my body, I reckon you should be a little less freaked out than me!"

"Does it hurt?"

"I'm managing the pain," April said. "But we're not going to get very far unless we fix this."

"Fix it? How the hell do we 'fix it?' Your bone's sticking out!"

"I was a nurse," April said slowly. "Before all this. I can tell you what to do."

Cotton stopped the 4Runner at the railroad tracks and let the engine idle.

"I need you to set up rear security," he said as he looked down the tracks.

In the distance, he could see the rail yard and, more specifically, the woods that ran alongside it. That would be his point of entry. First, he would set up an observation post at the highest point he could find to better understand what he was dealing with and then make entry once he had the lay of the land.

"Rear security?" Jean asked. "For what?"

"We don't know the composition of the enemy or what their security patrols look like. Last thing I need is someone coming up behind me while I'm in there."

Jean eyed her father for a moment and then shook her head. "Were you this bad a liar when you were in the Teams?"

"It's important!" Cotton insisted.

"I know what you're doing," Jean said. "So just stop it. You need a second gun in there more than you need someone at a random static security post."

"How do you even know what that is?" Cotton asked.

"Six-dash-five," Jean said with a smile, referencing the Marine Corps Rifle Squad manual.

"I now regret giving you that," Cotton said. "But

in all fairness, I didn't think you were actually going to read it."

"Well, I did," Jean said. "So I know when someone's trying to sideline me."

"This won't be like before," Cotton persisted. "These men are trained soldiers."

"Who've probably never been shot at," Jean said. "A deficit I'm fixing to rectify if they took April."

Cotton couldn't help but smile. "You're definitely my daughter."

The two walked quietly through the woods, effectively patrolling their way to a small wooded hill that overlooked the rail yard. Cotton gave Jean the hand signal to stop, and he dropped his pack. After she had also dropped hers, he performed a hasty 'box recon' of the area, checking for anyone who might have been posted in their immediate vicinity, but found no one.

These people had no reason to believe there was anyone in the area worth worrying about, so there was a distinct possibility security was going to be fairly lax. As far as the Poles knew, there was no one in the Texas Meat belt other than some random feudal kingdoms and ragtag groups of marauders.

Cotton returned to where Jean had set up a hasty observation post. She knelt beside her pack, watching the rail yard through binos.

"What have we got?" Cotton asked.

"Near as I can tell, it's about a platoon-sized force. Forty at best. See those railcars to the east of the main terminal?" Jean asked.

Cotton flipped up the magnifier on his DDM4 and looked through it. He wouldn't get the same kind of magnification Jean had on the binoculars, but he could still make out what she was indicating. "Yeah, I see them."

"Notice how they're locked up, but all the others around the yard are partially open?"

Damn, she's sharp.

"You're right," Cotton said. "Figure that's where they're holding prisoners?"

"Makes sense," Jean said. "But probably not many. Way you told it, they're not in the prisoner-taking business. But, for whatever reason, they took April, so that might be where she ended up."

"Leverage," Cotton said. "Americans don't do well with women being hurt. If they wanted to draw folks out for an ambush, that would be one way to do it."

Jean put down the binos and looked at her father. "Is that what you think this is? A trap?"

Cotton thought about it for a moment and then shook his head. "No," he said. "At least, not right now. For the moment, we have the element of surprise."

Jean looked at her watch. "Still got three hours before the sun goes down," she said. "In case you're thinking that might be the way to go."

"I want to," Cotton said, indicating that a night raid under NODs—night optical devices—would be ideal. "But I don't know if we have that kind of time. Notice how they're working on the other engines?"

"Didn't escape my attention," she said.

"They're fixing to move, and if it were me, I'd plan to do it before nightfall."

"Then we hit them now," Jean said decisively. "Those railcars are near the rear perimeter fence. We breach it, hit the cars one by one until we find her, and then get out."

"What if we don't find her?" Cotton said, testing his daughter. "What if she's not in those cars?"

"I know my limits," Jean said. "I'm brave but I ain't stupid. If we don't find her in those railcars we have to get out."

. . .

Jorge jogged back down the road to where Roland stood with Randall Eisler and Harris.

"I didn't find shit," Jorge said, visibly out of breath. "Some skid marks on the road, but not much aside from that."

"*Shit!*" Roland snapped. "This is fucking *bad*."

Randall Eisler raised an eyebrow. "Look, I don't mean to be insensitive here, and I know she did some good work for you, but are we missing something? Why is this Fred woman so important?"

"We weren't working much in the nineties. You remember that, right?" he asked Jorge.

"I wasn't in the Unit back then, but I know what you're talking about."

"Well, anything we could scoop up back then that was real world, it was a big deal. In '98, there was a high level meeting between a bunch of the Western nations on their nuclear programs. Some of us got pulled for protective details for some of the big wigs, but not the ones you'd think. The details were for the people *working* on the program, not deploying it. The ones it was real important they didn't fall into the wrong hands." Roland paused for a moment. "That was when I met Fred."

"Shit," Jorge said. He understood where this was going.

"I don't quite know how all this works," Roland went on, "but she was on the team that provided the encryption for the systems controlling our silos."

"And what are the chances they can still be accessed?" Harris interjected. "I doubt there was time to disable them."

"And probably no one cared," Randall Eisler said. "Little busy trying to keep their faces from getting eaten off."

"That's about the size of it," Roland said.

"How bad is it?" Jorge asked. "What could happen if the wrong people get a hold of her?"

"Ever tried standing in a tanning booth with no eye protection on?" Roland asked. "It's about that bad."

Something caught Harris's eye and he stared at it for a moment before he understood what he was looking at. "Marble City Rail Station," he said.

"What?" Roland asked, sounding slightly annoyed.

Harris walked across the road to a truck that was on its side. He pointed at the door where the words "Rail Station Maintenance Crew" were stenciled.

"You're kidding," Jorge said.

"Must've jacked the vehicles to increase their

mobility," Harris said. "Probably a safe bet that's where they took her."

Roland smiled. "You know, Harris, I didn't like you much when we met. I still don't, but I'm coming around."

"You can't scream," Fred said as she unbuckled her belt. "If they hear you, they'll know we're up to something and split us up."

"I'll do my best," April said.

"Not good enough," Fred said. "Take off your belt."

"What?" April asked.

"Just do it!"

April complied. It was clear that every movement she made was causing searing pain at the site of her injury, and she gritted her teeth accordingly. She removed her belt and handed it to Fred.

"I'm sorry," Fred said, "but you have to open your mouth."

"I was afraid you were going to say something like that."

April's belt was thinner than Fred's, and the older woman used it to gag April, wrapping it around her head until it was secure and she could fix the buckle. Next, Fred moved her hands to where the piece of bone was protruding from April's leg.

The woman had already given her detailed instruction on what to do, so now all she had to do was actually do it.

"Bite down hard!" Fred ordered.

April did as she was told and looked at the ceiling of the railcar. There was no other way.

Fred laid her belt down on the floor, took the back of April's ankle in one hand, and pulled, shoving the bone back in the direction it needed to go.

April was silent, but her body was tense, like a live wire. Fred didn't look at her because she knew if she saw the sheer agony on the woman's face, she might stop. Instead, she pushed until the bone was no longer visible, snatched up her belt, and wrapped it tightly around the injured area until she fixed it in place with the buckle.

Finally, she looked at April and saw the woman's eyes rolling back in her head. She was about to pass out.

"No!" Fred nearly shouted, and reaching out, she slapped April hard across the face. Like most things she did in the apocalypse, Fred was not one hundred percent sure what effect it would have, but she had seen enough people do it in movies that she figured it might work.

April's eyes snapped open, bulging with pain, and she stared accusingly back at Fred.

"Sorry," Fred replied sheepishly as she undid the belt from April's mouth. "It was the only thing I could think to do. You were about to lose consciousness."

"Bedside manner looks a lot different in the apocalypse," April lamented.

"How do you feel?" Fred asked.

"Weirdly fine," April said as he looked down at her leg. Aside from the blood soaking her pants and the tightly wound belt, she couldn't feel much of anything.

"That probably won't last," Fred said. "You're just high on adrenaline and cortisol."

Without warning, the door slid open, and two men jumped inside.

Fred spun and threw out her right hand.

"No!" she shouted. "Palm strike!"

The heel of her palm connected with the man's chin, snapping his head back and causing him to stumble backwards out of the railcar. While Fred had never hit anyone in her life, she had taken a women's assertiveness course twenty years prior, much of which had involved shouting "No!" and throwing palm strikes. The course had culminated in each attendee breaking a board and going home feeling very empowered.

For some reason, that training had burrowed itself deep into her psyche and chose this exact point in time to resurface. Unfortunately, it was no good against the next three soldiers who piled into the car and shoved her to the floor, zip-tying her once more.

April wanted to leap into the fray, but the ensuing pain from her injury rendered her little more than useless. She would just be beaten again, and it was questionable how much damage a woman with only one working leg could do to several large men.

Cotton and Jean stopped at the edge of the woods and looked toward the three railcars.

"Any bets on which one it is?" Cotton asked.

"I'll take the one on the right," Jean decided. "You take the other two."

"I think it's better if you cover while I hit them," Cotton said.

Jean set her jaw.

"Hey," Cotton said. "I'm right about this one. I

get it, you're the Sweet Valley Pipe Hitter but I've been at this a few days."

"'Sweet Valley?'" Jean asked in dismay.

"That reference might be before your time," Cotton said, "but I need you to roll with me on this one. I'm stronger, I can get the doors open faster, and I can go hands-on with anyone inside who might not be compliant."

"Okay," Jean said, coming around. "I'll set up between the cars so I've got some cover, and if anyone comes, I'll make it rain."

Cotton couldn't help but laugh a little. "Okay," he said. "But it's probably best if you don't go around repeating that last part."

General Zhukov walked in through the rear entrance of the small train station and tossed his notebook onto the desk of the small office he had taken over. The whole thing was a mess; every last bit of it. Not just the mission itself, or the Polish troops he had been given command of. No, it was the country itself, and everyone in it.

Really, it was quite unbelievable what had happened. Yes, the rest of the world had experienced problems with their vaccines, and while nearly every nation denied those side effects, it had eventually become accepted as part of the deal. If everyone wanted the damn virus to eventually go away, a certain percentage of the population was going to have to take it on the chin.

This meant some strange cancer clusters, some paralysis here and there, and, yes, there was some brain damage. However, even with all that, the rest of the world didn't experience the side effect the American vaccine had cultivated. Specifically, people eating each other.

It was just like something out of a bad movie. If Zhukov had his way—which he didn't—he would have just built an electrified fence around the whole country and been done with it, but the old guard from the Proletariat days had a way of never letting a grudge die. They wanted the land and its resources. More importantly, they wanted the bragging rights that the Russian Army had finally rolled across the purple mountain majesty in their armored columns and covered itself in glory.

As if any of it mattered. Even if this planned invasion from the north was successful, they would still eventually have to contend with the Chinese approaching from the west and the south. A patently ridiculous deal had been struck through the United

Nations that the Colorado Rockies would be the line of demarcation between the two burgeoning empires.

Zhukov laughed a little even thinking about that idea. For the first time in nearly a hundred years, not one but *two* ancient empires had a very real chance of actually conquering the world, and anyone who thought they would just give that up and play nice was worse than a fool. The idea that the U.N. held any sway over either party was also absurd, as the decisions made by the Secretary General were simply a matter of how much gold was being pushed his way. Though, as time went on, it was also becoming a matter of siding with whoever you thought was most likely to be the ultimate victor.

This last piece of business was one that Zhukov didn't like to think too much about, as any true student of military history knew it seemed fairly obvious who would be the victor in this struggle. The Chinese had taken India without a shot being fired. They had struck a deal early on with the military government of Pakistan and, seemingly in the blink of an eye, the size of their army had tripled. While Russia might have had the edge in technology and weapons—and even that was questionable—they could not compete with the raw numbers now being tallied by the Chinese.

Unless, of course, this bit of luck he had run into turned out to be true. When the idea had first been floated to run facial recognition scans on any prisoners they took, Zhukov had thought it sounded like a terrible waste of time. That is, until he seemed to have hit the proverbial jackpot.

He reached down and opened the notebook he had tossed onto the desk, then flipped to a page he had bookmarked and read the entry again. He had stumbled across intelligence that indicated there might be another scientist much like this woman Fred in the City State of Houston, a Doctor Gregory Wilson. Supposedly, this man was not only linked to the US nuclear program, but he was also connected to the company that had developed the Pandemify vaccine. It seemed like too much of a coincidence, and despite not wanting to journey further into this supposed 'Texas Meat Belt,' Zhukov knew he needed to follow up on it. Perhaps it would be a useful assignment for the Alpha Group positioned with the Third Division.

Zhukov picked up one of the blank dispatch forms that could be used to transmit messages back to the Third Motor Rifles Division and on to higher command. He thought for a moment about how much information he should disclose. He didn't want to risk sending unvetted intelligence and then looking like a fool if nothing came of it. After a moment, he decided just to send everything in a burst message, and he scrawled the relevant details onto the sheet.

As if on cue, the bells on the main door rang, and he turned to see a half dozen of the Poles dragging the woman in. One was trailing behind, covering a bloody mouth.

"Did the good professor give you a hard time?" Zhukov asked with a smile.

The Poles said nothing. They didn't like him and he didn't like them, and he had verbally acknowledged it early on in the campaign. He did not need them to like him, only to follow his orders.

"Go to hell!" Fred snapped.

"Is that what they teach at Oxford?" Zhukov asked as he reached out to one of the soldiers and handed him the dispatch form, with the understanding it should be sent immediately. He turned back to their captive and saw the surprise on her face. "Oh, yes, I was not being hyperbolic before when I said that we know who you are, Doctor Frederique Van Sant."

"I don't know what you're talking about," Fred said stoically.

"I also know you went through a short training course at the Farm when you took your government contract and that you understand how to resist interrogation at a basic level," Zhukov continued. "So I am capable of going far beyond basic if that is what you require."

Fred said nothing.

"I know that you wrote the base level code for the encryption system used by the US nuclear program." Fred tried not to give herself away with her facial expression, but Zhukov saw through it with little effort. "What you need to think about right now, is just what you're holding out for. What country are you trying to protect? America is gone. We are clearly here already, and the Chinese are not far behind. So, as near as I can tell, you only have one decision to make."

There was silence for a moment.

"And what is that?" Fred asked.

Zhukov smiled. "Do you want to speak Russian or Chinese?"

CHAPTER 7

COTTON WANTED to turn back and check on how Jean was doing, but he knew it would be wasted energy and was more likely to slow them down than provide any benefit. He was rapidly learning that he needed to trust the young girl. Yes, she was only fifteen, but she knew what she was doing. He should have known that better than anyone because he was the one who had taught her nearly everything she knew. The other lessons had been learned more recently—and paid for in blood.

They had managed to cut through the chain link fence fairly quickly using a breach pen, which was lucky given the disposable cutting tool only burned for about thirty seconds. Cotton wasn't happy about having to use the device, but he had been saving it for a rainy day, and at the moment, it was damn pouring.

So far, no one seemed to have taken any notice of them. Unbelievably, there were only two guards standing at the front gate, both oriented outward, and neither had turned around in the past five minutes. Realistically, there was no reason for them to turn and look back into the rail yard, as there was no reason to think anyone would be coming at them from within.

Cotton had switched rifles with Jean as his DDM4 was suppressed and had a magnifier. In the unlikely event one of the guards turned in his direction, she would execute both of them, and though the rifle was not truly 'silent,' it would buy them enough time to get back out the way they came before half of the Polish army was on top of them.

Cotton moved stealthily as he came around the front of the first railcar and pulled the door open.

"Help me!"

A man emerged from the railcar and was on top of him, his hands bound. Cotton reacted without thinking; he slammed his fist into the man's face, knocking him out cold on the floor of the railcar.

"Shit," Cotton said under his breath.

"They've seen us," he heard Jean say from between the railcars. "I'm doing it."

Cotton didn't reply as he moved to the next car.

Jean sat in a half-kneeling position between the two cars and scanned the rail yard. The men were about one hundred yards away. A shot like that was child's play with the EOTech reticle, but she knew not to get sloppy. She settled the center dot on the first man's face. He was looking right at her, but his brain clearly had not yet registered what he was seeing.

Jean exhaled as she took up the slack on the Geissele trigger and broke the wall. There was the subdued *pop* of the rifle and the metallic sound of the bolt cycling. Normally, she didn't hear that while shooting, but the Deadair Sandman suppressed the shot enough that the *clank* was audible.

The dead Pole dropped to the ground as Jean traversed her optic to the second guard and repeated the same procedure. Another *clank*, and she could feel and smell the blowback of the hot gasses on her face.

This man also collapsed.

"They're down," Jean said. "We have no time."

Cotton yanked back the door of the second railcar. No screaming man this time, no nothing. He almost moved to the second one, but something stopped him. Instead, he hopped inside and activated his white light.

April was inside. She was passed out on the floor in a pool of slick blood. It looked like someone had applied a tourniquet of some sort to her leg. Without another wasted moment, Cotton scooped her up and hopped back out of the railcar.

"Let's go!" he urged.

"Still working," Jean said as she dropped two more soldiers who had just come around the corner of the main building and were about to nearly trip over the two dead men at the gate.

Jean stood back up and followed her father toward the rear fence.

Cotton laid April on the ground and was ready to slip through the fence when her eyes fluttered open.

"It's okay!" Jean said quickly, putting a hand on the woman. "We're getting you out of here!"

"No!" April nearly shouted. "You can't!"

"You're in shock," Cotton said as he pulled the opening in the fence a little wider. "It's fine. You're safe now."

"*No!*" April repeated. "There was a woman with me. The one from Cypress Mill!"

That got Cotton's attention. "What are you talking about?"

"She was with me in the railcar. The woman who arrived with Jorge."

"I'm sorry," Cotton said. "We don't have time for her. This place is about to turn into the ending of *Red Dawn*."

"They're trying to get control of the nuclear arsenal!" April snapped.

"What?" Jean asked.

"That woman worked on some program for the government. If they have her, they can break the codes!"

"You've got to be *shitting* me," Cotton said, the exhaustion in his voice obvious. "What the hell else can go wrong?"

"You have to help her!" April demanded.

Cotton looked through the space between the two railcars to where the main terminal lay. "I can't believe I'm doing this," he said under his breath as he traded rifles with his daughter again.

"I'll get April to the tree line," Jean said. "You can count on me."

. . .

"Stop!" Harris said as he sat in the passenger seat and held the binos to his eyes.

Jorge complied and rolled the truck off to the side of the road.

"What have you got?" Roland asked from the back of the truck, where he sat with Randall Eisler.

"Sentry in the road with a makeshift barricade," Harris said. "And it looks like the main gate is probably three hundred meters to his rear."

The four men had commandeered the rail yard truck as they had assumed—correctly—that anyone who saw it approaching from a distance would think it was part of the ambush contingent returning to the forward operating base.

"What's the play?" Jorge asked, looking through the open rear window to where Roland sat with his AR.

"Hey-diddle-diddle," Roland replied, implying that they would just ram the main gate.

"Sure you don't want to try something a little more tactical?" Jorge asked. "Maybe flank through the woods?"

"You ain't gonna believe this," Roland said, "but I know this place. I worked here for a summer, unloading boxcars when I was sixteen."

"No shit?" Randall Eisler asked.

Roland shrugged. "For such a big place, Texas is a pretty small world," he said. "And that's how I know the best way to do this is to just blaze through the front gate. On the right, we'll have the fueling stations, and on the left, we'll have the main terminal. I also figure these guys probably can't shoot for shit, so if we're going fast enough, they're not gonna hit us."

"Scorched earth?" Jorge asked, implying they would effectively just hit the ground with all guns blazing.

"I don't know a better way," Roland said.

Cotton moved in a wide loop toward what looked like some sort of refueling station beside the main gate. It seemed like poor planning to position something with such potential for creating a large explosion so near to the entrance, and an even worse option for cover and concealment, but it was also the only choice he had.

While there were a few other small buildings around the rail yard, the main terminal seemed like the most likely place for the Poles to be holding the woman. Cotton thought for a moment about the best way to handle the situation.

Tactically, he knew what he should do. The moment she came into sight, he should put a round into her. It sounded cold—and it was—but it was also the best option for eliminating the supposed threat to the nuclear arsenal and getting him, Jean, and April out of this place alive.

If he was able to keep Fred in one piece and get her out without risking Jean's safety, he would, but otherwise the priority had to be keeping her out of enemy hands.

The whole thing was unreal. Cotton remembered when he was a boy and the Soviets were still the boogeyman in the closet. He would watch *Red Dawn* with his father and imagine being out there in the woods fighting the Commies on American soil.

Now, it was really happening, but it didn't feel at all like he had thought it would. He had no intention of going head-to-head with the Russians the way Patrick Swayze and Charlie Sheen had. He just wanted to get this over with and get his daughter to safety.

Cotton felt the zip of a round pass directly in front of his face. He dropped to a knee and spun to his right, picking up the threat only twenty meters away. It was a lone soldier who had spotted him and decided to try his luck, but he was about to be found wanting.

Cotton put a sixty-two grain round through the soldier's throat and then sprang back to his feet, continuing his loop past the edge of the refueling station and toward the terminal. There was no reason to stay and watch the man die.

Across the yard, Cotton saw the door to one of the buildings swing open and soldiers began pouring out. Someone had finally taken notice of the dead bodies littering the area by the front gate and had decided to take action.

There was no more time for finesse, so Cotton moved in a straight line for the terminal building, unloading suppressive fire on the men who were coming at him as he moved.

"Can you make that shot from here?" April asked as she watched Jean adjust her prone position behind the MK18 short barrel rifle.

The girl had used her pack to set up a hasty firing position and was now looking through the red dot sight at the position roughly three hundred meters below her.

"Only one way to find out," Jean said as she flicked off the safety and began taking up the slack on the trigger. "Just be ready to feed me when I go dry."

April picked up two of the AR magazines Jean had laid out and waited. She also took the opportunity to further tighten the belt on her leg. Getting up the hill had been beyond painful, but she knew if she kept the belt tight, she could keep going. The moment it started to go slack in the least, April could feel things moving around and her pain levels skyrocketed.

Once the shooting had started in the yard below, the two women had stopped and Jean had seen the door to the building swing open and the Polish soldiers begin streaming out. There were too many of them, even for her father, and she knew it. She also knew she couldn't just sit there and watch him die.

It was an impossible shot on a simple Aimpoint red dot without a magnifier, or at least it should have been for a twelve-year-old girl who had only ever spent a handful of hours on an actual rifle range. And that had just been because her father thought it would be 'fun,' not because he'd ever imagined she might need to use those skills in the real world.

Jean recited the fundamentals to herself and remembered what her father always said. *If you adhere to the fundamentals, you can always make the shot.*

"Please, God," she whispered. "Give me this."

The first shot broke, and Jean watched a man fall to the ground. Two others turned in her direction and brought their weapons up. She fired five more shots in rapid succession, and one of the men face-planted into the gravel. With a little bit of skill and a whole lot of luck, she was making hits.

Now that Jean knew she was on target, she took the brakes off and began a steady, staccato rhythm of rapid, controlled fire.

Cotton smiled as he watched the soldiers literally running in circles, taking fire from two different directions. He could see the glint from Jean's optic on the hill above.

That girl's making shots at three hundred meters with a damn red dot. He'd clearly taught her well.

With no more time to waste, Cotton darted across the open yard and found what he was looking for: the side entrance into the main terminal. He snapped one leg out in front of him and kicked it open, entering the room with his weapon up. The three soldiers inside seemed to still be trying to understand what was going on outside, but that understanding would come far too late.

Cotton hit the first two with controlled pairs, dropping them where they stood. The third at least managed to get a shot off but was nowhere near hitting his mark, and he was rewarded with a rifle round through his abdomen.

Cotton continued crossing the room and sent another round through the third soldier's head. He entered an adjoining space, where he found a much older man sitting across a table from Fred. He wore general's stars on his epaulets, and Cotton recognized his uniform as being Russian, not Polish.

The man reached for something on his belt.

"Don't do it!" Cotton shouted. "Two fingers, out of the holster!"

Zhukov nodded his understanding and complied, lifting the MP-443 Grach pistol from its holster with his thumb and index finger.

"Toss it!" Cotton snapped. He kept his rifle trained on Zhukov as he looked around the room.

"You're out of your depth," Zhukov said calmly. "There's no way you can get out of here."

"Toss that fucking sidearm!" Cotton shouted.

Zhukov complied and threw the pistol across the room. Whoever this man was, the general would not be able to bargain with him. This much was obvious.

"And you've got that backwards," Cotton said. "You ain't walking out of here." He looked to Fred. "Up. We're leaving."

Fred stood up quickly and walked over to Cotton.

"I have a hundred men stationed here," Zhukov said. "You need to listen to me."

Cotton looked out the window and saw more men pouring out of the adjacent buildings.

"Shit." He turned to Fred. "Grab that pistol he just tossed."

Fred ran across the room and scooped up the firearm. "We're not making it out of here, are we?" she asked.

Cotton stared at her coldly for a moment and then shook his head.

"Holy shit!" Jorge shouted as they bore down on the gate. "This plan just went from bad to worse! I've got at least two dozen hostiles on open ground, about fifty meters past the gate."

The former Unit member had set himself up in the rear of the truck, with his recce rifle positioned over the cabin. Through the VUDU 1-8 scope, he could see the soldiers running across the rail yard.

"Are we still doing this?" Harris asked, turning to Roland beside him in the cabin.

"No other option!" Roland replied, and he brought up his AR, ready to fire through the windshield.

Roland could see the fear in Harris's eyes. Things had just gotten very real, real fast.

"Just drive!" Roland said. "Don't think about it! You hit that gate like it smacked your Mama, and we'll take care of the rest.

Harris could hear the steady *pop*s of Jorge's rifle overhead as the man began taking well-aimed shots at the soldiers inside the rail yard, and as they moved closer, Randall Eisler joined in. The latter didn't have Jorge's young eyes or the man's magnified scope, but once they were close enough, he put his Holosun red dot where he needed his rounds to go and hoped God would take care of the rest.

As the gate drew closer, Roland buckled his seat belt and braced his feet against the floor. He flicked his weapon off safe and let out a breath, then began firing.

"*Down!*" Cotton shouted and tackled Fred to the floor as rounds began tearing through the room, shattering every pane of glass and sending shards of wood splintering through the air.

It all seemed to happen at once. A truck rammed the front gate with what seemed like several guns firing at the same time, and the soldiers flooding the yard began cutting loose on anything they didn't recognize.

Cotton turned and saw Zhukov crawling away from him.

"Stay here!" Cotton ordered Fred as he slid across the floor away from her.

He wasn't sure who this general was, but it was a safe assumption that if they were actually going to get out of this mess alive, Cotton might have a few questions for him.

Cotton quickly overtook Zhukov, careful not to pop his head up too much as rounds were still tearing the room apart. Whoever was in that truck had decided it was a good idea to engage the Polish troops directly through the windows of the terminal building.

Zhukov could feel Cotton grabbing at his boots and flipped over to kick him off, but this provided Cotton the opportunity he needed to quickly scoot atop Zhukov and begin raining elbows down on him.

The older man was clearly no slouch in the combatives department, as he worked himself into a side-lying position beneath Cotton and managed to counter with a series of strikes to the former SEAL's ribs.

Cotton knew immediately he had screwed up. He'd seen a man who was significantly older than him and seemed to be a little paunchy around the edges and had made an assumption that he would be an easy victory.

He was wrong.

Zhukov was strong; a hell of a lot stronger than he looked. The man also clearly had some training in grappling, as he locked his legs around Cotton and began driving his hips up. Cotton realized what was happening.

The general was trying to drive the younger man up into the crossfire that was shredding the room around them.

. . .

Harris could feel his heart racing, beating out of his chest, as his vision narrowed. He was doing his best to control the sympathetic nervous system response, but to no avail. He had dropped to a crouched position beside a parked railcar and was engaging what looked like an entire squad of the Polish soldiers. He knew that Roland, Jorge, and Randall Eisler had taken up other firing positions around the yard after they'd exited the truck, but it sure felt a hell of a lot like he was out there on his own.

Harris had trusted that Roland had some kind of deeper plan beyond simply ramming the front gate and going toe-to-toe with the soldiers in the rail yard, but he was starting to suspect that wasn't the case. It was very possible that the former Development Group SEAL simply liked the fight and was perhaps continually trying to up the ante.

Harris could also see that Jorge had a switch that was very easily flipped, and though he might not have been looking for a fight the way Roland seemed to be, once things kicked off, the former Unit member was clearly right at home.

To further complicate matters, there also seemed to be a shooter on the hill overlooking the rail yard, and it wasn't one hundred percent clear whether they were friendly, as most of their shots were hitting the dirt, and the ones that didn't, while they were striking the Polish soldiers, could have been accidental.

"*Feed me!*" Jean shouted.

April reached out with an AR mag and Jean snatched it, switching out the empty in her MK18. A small contingent of the Polish soldiers had opened a rear gate and were heading for her position. At this point, they had realized they were being fired upon from an elevated position.

If the soldiers had had any ideas about fleeing the fight, they knew that after the truck hit the front entrance, that would no longer be an option, so they needed to clear a path out the rear. The problem with that idea was that little Jean Wiley and her MK18 were 'making it rain,' as her father liked to say.

"Looks like they've decided to come to me," Jean said as she watched the soldiers doing their best to sprint up the hill toward her position.

As the men began to close the three-hundred-meter gap, Jean took several more well-aimed shots, now only working in the two-hundred-meter range, close enough that she could be assured of clean, center mass hits.

Several more soldiers were flooding through the opening in the rear gate, and Jean could see they were now remembering their basic infantry training and were employing a fire team rush "*I'm up, they see me, I'm down*" strategy.

"Damn!" Jean snapped, and she rolled up into a half-kneeling position as the men closed in. She reached down, drew her Glock 19 pistol from its holster, and handed it to April. "There's too many, and they know where we are. We have to move."

"But Cotton's still down there!" April protested.

"Don't you think I know that?" Jean shouted as she focused again on her optic and took three more shots, but the men were zig-zagging so fast up the hill that she wasn't getting any hits. "But if we stay here, we die. There's a draw down the side of the hill there. We can follow that back into the woods. They won't be able to find us there."

"What then?"

"We wait this thing out until the shooting stops and then circle back."

. . .

"They're skinning out!" Jorge shouted from his firing position atop one of the railcars.

There were still a respectable number of the Polish soldiers staying in the fight, but the tide had clearly turned, and Jorge had already noticed a number of them trying to escape out the back. Either that or they were trying to go after whoever was giving them hell from up on that hill. Either way, it meant fewer shooters in the rail yard proper.

Roland had been shooting and moving throughout the yard, rabbiting from one structure to another and killing the enemy as he went. From what Jorge could see, both Randall Eisler and Harris had also been holding their own.

In the midst of it all, the former Delta soldier couldn't shake the feeling that this was the beginning of a 'new normal.' Over the past eighteen months, there hadn't really been much in the way of serious fighting. There was the odd skirmish with a loosely organized group of marauders that didn't want to fall in line with Roland's plan or other things of that nature, but nothing like this. Now, they had been active participants in two major conflicts in as many days, not even counting what had happened at Tow and Cypress Mill.

Up on the hill to his rear, Jorge could hear shooting, and he knew that the soldiers had probably made it to the top. He sat up from his prone position, transitioned to sitting, and contorted his body to be able to angle the recce rifle up enough to take some shots.

Jean turned and fired what remained in her magazine before hitting a speed reload. Beside her, April also stopped and unloaded the Glock on several of the dozen soldiers sprinting toward them across the open ground.

Jean let the bolt in her SBR fly forward and brought her weapon back up, but there was only a gap of a couple dozen feet. She couldn't miss, but that meant the approaching soldiers couldn't, either.

"I'll do it if you want me to!" April said, and Jean knew what she meant. The woman was willing to turn the pistol on Jean and then on herself to avoid being captured.

"I—"

Jean's sentence was cut short as one of the men stumbled forward and hit the ground with a hole in his chest.

He had stumbled forward. *Someone shot him from behind!*

"*Fight!*" Jean screamed as she began hammering

rounds toward the advancing soldiers and watched two more drop from fire unleashed by the unknown sniper.

Within seconds, there were only two left, but they were too close and both men tackled Jean, almost seeming not to notice April standing there.

April put her pistol to one man's head and pulled the trigger, evacuating his brains from his cranium. She tried to pull the trigger again at the second man, only to realize her slide was locked back. In a moment of sheer desperation, she lunged forward and slammed the butt of the pistol into the temple of the soldier straddling Jean.

The man was momentarily stunned and rolled onto his side, with April quickly on top of him. She repeatedly slammed the butt of the empty pistol into his face.

"*Reload!*" Jean shouted as she tossed the magazine that had been in her belt to April.

The woman caught it. She dropped the empty magazine, slammed the fresh one into the magazine well, sent the slide forward, leveled it with the Polish soldier's face, and pulled the trigger.

. . .

Cotton could hear that the shooting had died down, but he still faced the problem of being locked in Zhukov's grip. His arms were also trapped in the Sambo hold the man had him in, which meant he couldn't get to the pistol on his right hip. And Zhukov was slowly working him into what looked like some bastardized version of a Brazilian jiu-jitsu triangle choke.

Holy shit! Cotton thought to himself. *This old guy is going to choke me out!*

It was true that General Mikhail Zhukov was a Sambo player going back several decades, ever since he was a boy growing up in Eastern Ukraine, long before he'd ever even had aspirations of becoming a military man. Not only that, but he had been one of those young men who felt the need to test himself on the streets of Odessa by learning what it took to translate his skills to a real fight against men who had nothing to lose.

General Zhukov knew nothing about the bearded man who had stormed the terminal before all the shooting started, but what he did know was that this man had picked the wrong fight.

Cotton felt Zhukov's leg begin to slip around his head and his grip tightening on the former SEAL's arm as he pulled it downward. The triangle was closing, and Cotton had no time to find a way out of it.

Then he felt something: a tugging on his belt. Zhukov's eyes widened as he looked past Cotton to something behind him.

The *pop* was deafening.

Cotton reflexively closed his eyes as the blood hit his face. He felt Zhukov's grip go limp, and he rolled free of the man's grasp. Then his brain processed what had happened, and he looked up at Fred standing over him and holding his Glock 17. She had pulled it from his holster and shot Zhukov dead with it.

Cotton rolled up into a stooped position and held out his hand to her. The woman was clearly in some degree of shock, and he knew she needed to be handled with kid gloves.

"You did good," Cotton said. "Now, give it here."

Fred's eyes were almost glazed over, staring into the hole she had made in Zhukov's head. Cotton's hollow point nine millimeter ammo had done quite a number on what used to be the general's face.

Cotton stood up, his hand still held out to her. "Hey!" he snapped.

Fred turned to him quickly, as if she hadn't

known he was there. Just as quickly, she held out the pistol to him, and he took it.

"I meant what I said," Cotton said. "You did good."

"On the floor! Now!"

Cotton turned to the sound of the voice barking orders and began to bring the pistol up, but he stopped as he registered who he was looking at.

Roland Reese slowed to a stop and looked at Cotton with a confused expression on his face. "What in God's name are you doin' here, Cotton?"

Jorge walked across the rail yard with a broad smile on his face. The man had clearly been physically taxed sprinting up the hill that overlooked the yard, but he was happy to see Cotton Wiley.

"Good to see you!" Jorge said. "How the hell did you end up here?"

"Same way you did," Cotton said. "First looking for April—and then for her."

Fred said nothing. She looked around the open yard at the dozens of dead bodies. This was all her fault, or at least she thought it was.

"Anything up there?" Cotton asked, indicating the hill.

"Nah," Jorge replied. "Just a lot of fucked-up Polish soldiers. Someone was up there giving us a hand, but it looks like they hightailed it out of Dodge."

"It was Jean and April," Cotton said, the concern in his voice obvious. "I need to get up there."

"I'm sorry," Jorge said, "but they're long gone. I went all the way into the woods. There's no trace."

"Look, I'm glad I was able to help with whatever the hell this was," Cotton said, "but I have to go."

"Wait a minute," Jorge reasoned. "Think about it. You raised a smart girl. She's heading somewhere, right? You had some kind of rally point established, didn't you?"

Cotton thought about it. "No rally point. I ... I should have—"

Jorge stopped the train of thought before it started. "Okay. It's fine. Jean knows you're with us, and she knows we're headed for Oatmeal. That's where she'll go."

"And what if she doesn't?" Cotton asked. "What if she's out there in those woods, waiting for me?"

"That girl just killed half the fucking Polish Army from that hilltop. Trust me, she ain't waitin' around for *anyone* to save her."

Cotton didn't like the idea of taking this kind of

risk, but he also knew it was the one most likely to pay off. Jorge was right; Jean wouldn't remain static. She would be moving, just like he'd taught her.

Harris looked back to where Jorge, Roland, and Cotton were all standing outside the main terminal. How the hell had Cotton circled back around to them again?

"Hey!" Randall Eisler snapped. "Pay attention."

"Right," Harris said, and he turned back to the three Polish soldiers standing beside the railcar.

The men had all survived the assault and been summarily rounded up and zip-tied, but for what, no one knew. Harris figured they would probably just end up killing them, as the apocalypse wasn't quite the place for taking prisoners and managing their day-to-day lives. Of course, there was also the part where they were still cannibals, and judging by their appearance, the Polish soldiers were not. The math on that was pretty easy to figure out.

"Don't eyeball me, boy!" Randall Eisler snapped at one of the Polish soldiers, who was doing his best to stare him down, all the while wiggling around like he needed to use the restroom. "You got ants in your pants or something?"

Harris turned back to the scene at the terminal. What were the others talking about? He felt like he was being left out of something important.

"I'm talking to you!" Randall Eisler said, stepping forward.

The Polish soldier stepped into Randall Eisler's advance, produced a knife from behind his back, and stabbed the man directly in the side of the neck. Blood spraying from the wound, Eisler stumbled backward, grasping for the knife.

Harris brought his AR up and shot the Polish soldier, then turned and executed the other two as they attempted to make a break for it. He turned and saw Randall Eisler lying in the gravel and dirt, blood steadily pumping from his neck.

Harris reached back and pulled his IFAK from the Micro Trauma Now kit mounted to the back of his belt. He pulled a pack of gauze from the kit, ripped open the plastic covering, and packed the wound in Randall Eisler's neck, but the gauze was quickly soaked through. Randall Eisler was as white as a sheet, and it was clear the man was trying to say something but couldn't get the words out.

"Stop," Jorge said calmly as he took a knee beside Harris and pulled the man's hand back. "You can't do anything here."

Randall Eisler's eyes moved to the big man. He had heard what he said.

"There has to be *something* we can do!" Harris blurted. He looked up to where Cotton and Roland were standing over him, summoned by the shots. Neither man said anything.

"Sometimes there ain't nothing to do," Jorge said.

He reached down and took Randall Eisler's hand and waited until the man's eyes closed forever.

INTERLUDE TWO

It wasn't the way they had thought it would be. In fact, it wasn't anything close to what nearly every man in the Russian military had thought an event like this would be. In every war-game scenario, the invasion of America had been a prolonged war, most likely lasting years, with millions of Russian soldiers lost and a slow grind of pitched battles culminating in the destruction of Washington D.C. and the fall of the once powerful empire.

Instead, the Russian Ground Forces had lost sixty-five men. In the three weeks since they had crossed the northern border of the United States, the Russian Army had lost exactly sixty-five soldiers, and most of those had been accidental deaths, such as negligent discharges of firearms, falling off the backs of vehicles, drowning during a river crossing, etc.

Aside from a handful of run-ins with some relatively disorganized resistance, there really hadn't been much fighting at all. Now, the Third Motor Rifle Division was camped out in Central Texas, squarely between Houston and Austin. This was supposed to have been the campaign during which the division would finally cover itself in glory, and yet the campaign so far had been a complete disaster in terms of accumulating battle experience. The only logical explanation was that most of the remaining American forces had moved to the south to prepare a desperate last stand.

After all, they couldn't really all be gone, could they? Everyone had heard about the cannibals and the rumors that most of America was now deserted; that everyone lived in these supposed City States. The Russian forces were relatively close to one of the biggest, Houston. There should have been somebody out there, but they had yet to find them.

Now, Colonel Andrya Nikitin stood on the eastern edge of the military encampment, staring out into nothing.

The Colonel's adjutant, Lieutenant Volkov,

approached him from behind. "Colonel?" Volkov asked.

Nikitin looked over his shoulder and smiled. Volkov was one of the good ones, particularly considering that the army had been greatly expanded with conscripts. It was true that service had always been mandatory for young men, but it had only been a twelve-month term, and not many complained about that. Now, national service was six years or for the duration, whichever was longest. Nikitin knew which of the two it would be.

"Any word from General Zhukov?" Nikitin asked. "Or our U.N. puppets?"

Volkov laughed at the not-so-inside joke and shook his head. "Still nothing." He hesitated for a moment. "Should we send a detachment to Marble Falls? Is it possible they ran into some sort of trouble out there?"

"Their mandate is simple," Nikitin said. "Kill cannibals and collect intelligence. Honestly, I don't know what the point of their mission is. From the looks of things, we'll reach the Mexico border with no resistance."

"It's happened much faster than we thought," Volkov agreed. "The planners thought that in the best-case scenario, it would take six months of hard fighting to make it this far."

"Your point?" Nikitin asked sharply. Even if Volkov was one of the good ones, he was getting dangerously close to questioning his superiors.

"It's just that we know the Chinese have established forward operating bases in Mexico. We're not going to cross that line, are we?"

Nikitin thought about it for a moment. "That is not our decision," he said firmly.

"Lieutenant!" a voice shouted from behind the two men. Both turned to see a runner approaching them with a sheet of paper. "This burst transmission just came in from General Zhukov!"

Nikitin took the paper and looked at it. "Just now?" he asked.

"It was sent over an hour ago," the runner said, "but the atmospheric disturbance is playing havoc with our frequencies."

"What does it say?" Lieutenant Volkov asked and then caught himself. "If I may ask."

"It says that the General has intelligence relating to control of the American nuclear arsenal," Nikitin said slowly. "They have captured some scientist who understands how to access it."

"Could this be true?"

"It must be," Nikitin concluded. "General Zhukov is not a man given to flights of fancy. If he has sent this message, he has already vetted it in his own mind a thousand times over."

"Perhaps, then, the Chinese will not be so much of a problem after all?" Volkov mused.

"Perhaps," Nikitin concurred. "Have we received further contact from Zhukov?"

"No, Colonel. The—"

"Yes, yes," Nikitin replied dismissively to the runner. "I know. The atmospherics." He turned to Volkov. "Is the Alpha Group still training in the south?"

'Yes, Colonel," Volkov confirmed.

The Alpha Group was a sub-unit of the Spetsnaz, the Russian Special Forces. They were the best of the best, the equivalent of the U.S. Seal Team Six.

"Re-route them to Marble Falls," Nikitin said. "Have them assess the railyard there. If Zhukov is there, they can link up with him and ensure his safe return."

"And if he isn't?" Volkov asked.

"Pursue whatever leads are available."

Volkov turned to the runner, who clearly understood what message to relay. As if on cue, Volkov's radio squawked. He picked it up and waited as a message was relayed.

"What is it?" Nikitin asked.

Volkov looked past his commanding officer to the road ahead of them and simply pointed.

A woman was walking toward them in the distance ahead.

Nikitin looked at her for a moment and then turned back to Volkov.

The adjutant shrugged. "All they say is that a woman is coming from the south."

"This is ridiculous," Nikitin said. He turned back to the woman and watched her walking down the road toward them. "I will walk to her."

Nikitin walked down the same road at a brisk pace. Whoever this woman was, she was about to get the surprise of her life, walking into a Russian infantry encampment in the middle of Texas.

As he drew closer, Nikitin began to notice that something was wrong with the woman. There was a strangeness to her gait and the way in which her eyes locked onto his. Then he saw that it was more than just *how* she was looking at him. Her eyes were black, like twin orbs of coal hammered into her face, and steam was rising from her body.

Nikitin drew the sign of the cross before him

without even thinking about it and slowed to a halt. "Stop!" he shouted.

The woman continued her advance.

He reached down and unclipped his holster. He then looked over his shoulder to where Volkov stood. The lieutenant suddenly seemed very far away. The encampment was even further, at least a thousand meters down the road.

Nikitin pulled the radio from his belt and keyed it. "Volkov, are you receiving?"

Nikitin was shaken, and his nerves had caused him to forget his radio protocol.

"*Yes, Colonel,*" his adjutant's voice came back.

"Don't let anyone come out here," Nikitin said. "I will deal with her."

June Kennedy stopped in the road, only a dozen feet from Colonel Nikitin. She looked past him to the encampment and the men gathered there. She smiled. Her summer dress was in tatters, and it was smeared with blood and gore. She imagined she was quite a sight.

"Well," June said quietly, "you've just made yourself right at home, haven't you?"

"What ... are you?" Nikitin asked.

June smiled. "The future."

Nikitin kept his hand resting on the butt of his

pistol, but he was careful not to do anything to provoke the woman.

"And I'm not alone," June continued.

Nikitin felt the ground rumble beneath him, almost as if he were standing on train tracks. Then his radio chirped to life.

"Colonel! Colonel!" Volkov's voice shouted from the other side. *"We have contact! From all sides!"*

Nikitin turned and felt his body grow cold as he watched the horde racing across the landscape before him. There were hundreds—no, *thousands* of men and women running toward the encampment. The gunfire started; everything from rifles to machine guns. Then mortars began to engage, but the cannibals were already too close. They crashed into the Third Motor Rifle Division like waves against the shore.

Colonel Nikitin watched his men being overwhelmed by what he could only describe as a demonic force. He turned back to June Kennedy, drew his weapon, and pointed it at her.

The woman simply shook her head.

June snatched the pistol from his hand and held it casually by her side.

"That is not the way this will end," she said hauntingly.

CHAPTER 8

Then

"IT DIDN'T FALL," Cotton said as he stood beside his father and observed the Eastern Redbud tree on the border of their property. It had been split down the middle by a lightning strike. The trunk was still smoking, but the tree stood strong.

"That's the way with trees," Earl Wiley said as he drew off his hand-rolled cigarette and felt the cold winter wind hit him in the face.

Cotton looked up at his father. Earl Wiley was a bear of a man, just like his father before him, and just like his own father—Cotton's grandfather—he bore the scars of a life spent in the service of his country. He looked down at his son.

Cotton felt his father's eyes on him, and he looked to the old man and the scar that crossed his face in a diagonal fashion. "I don't know what that means," he said.

"What's that now?" Earl asked.

"The way with trees, I mean."

"Trees don't care," Earl clarified. "They can be struck by lightning, cut up for firewood, or left to their own devices. Trees don't care either way. They'll just keep being trees. They have zero sway for the machinations of man."

"'Zero sway?'"

Earl took another draw off his cigarette and smiled. "Got a lot of questions, don't you, boy?"

Cotton said nothing. He knew his father was a hard man because the world had made him that way, but he was also fair.

"Branches may sway, but the tree don't," Earl went on. "Not the trunk. People make that mistake. They think the tree sways, but it don't. We could learn a valuable lesson from the trees. Once you figure out your core values, you don't deviate. Not ever. Just like the trees. Zero sway."

Now

Cotton looked at himself in the mirror of the main terminal bathroom. He had found a pair of old clippers and some shaving supplies in a locker and had gone to work. Now, his head and his face were clean. It was a ritual he had adopted before going into battle; one he had started long ago. He remembered as a boy listening to his father and grandfather talking about their time at war, about Vietnam and World War Two. Grandpa Wiley had told him once that when the Marines landed at Guadalcanal, during what would become known as the 'Island Hopping Campaign' of World War Two, they had shaved their heads. In the beginning, it had been to avoid lice, but later on, it had become like their war paint. It was a way of becoming more animal than human; more war than peace.

Cotton set the clippers down and looked at the tattoos on his fingers.

ZERO SWAY.

He would find his daughter. No matter what.

. . .

"He's been in there a while," Jorge said as he stood in the main terminal with Roland. "You think he's okay?"

"He'll be fine," Roland said as he rifled through the paperwork in the small office Zhukov had been using. "I'll bet dollars to donuts he walks out of there with a shaved head and a new sense of purpose."

"Shaved head?" Jorge asked.

"At half-speed Cotton was better than most," Roland said. "I think he was already having problems with all the explosive breaching we were doing early on in the war, never mind all the training. I could tell when he started slowing down because he'd talk a little more slowly, let his hair grow out, start drinking more. Then one day it would be like someone flipped a switch and recharged his batteries. He'd shave his head, trim his beard and have a new sense of purpose."

"Did you ever doubt it?" Jorge asked. "The mission?"

Roland looked up from the desk. "What makes you ask that?"

"Not sure," Jorge said with a shrug. "Been thinking about it more lately. Maybe thinking about the time we lost. If it was all worth it."

"If I'm being honest, I never believed in it to

begin with," Roland said. "At least, not the way a lot of guys did. Not the way they wanted us to."

"Then why do it?"

"I got lucky," Roland said. "Early on, back in the nineties when most guys were just spinning their wheels doing log PT and other bullshit, I went to Six right away and started deploying. Killed my first man in Kosovo. Three of 'em, actually."

"You liked it, didn't you?" Jorge said.

"No," Roland replied. "I fucking *loved* it. Right there, I knew what my purpose was; what I wanted to do. I knew I was a killer. I just had to wait a few more years for the opportunity to *really* present itself."

The door to the bathroom opened and Cotton walked out, his head shaved and his beard trimmed.

Jorge smiled.

"Anything?" Cotton asked.

"Not much," Roland said. "Looks like they were pretty tight with their intel."

Cotton turned to Jorge, and as he did so, Roland slowly slid Zhukov's notebook off the desk and into his back pocket. Cotton watched it happen in the reflection of a mirror behind the main counter, but said nothing.

"How's Harris?" Cotton asked Jorge.

"Got him doing some imaginary SSE out in the yard," Jorge said, indicating a sensitive sight exploitation search. "He'll be fine."

"We should get back on the road," Cotton said. "I figure if these guys don't report in to wherever their command post is, someone's going to come looking eventually."

"Roger that," Roland said with a smile, and he walked toward the door.

There was something there, something off, but Cotton couldn't put his finger on it. He turned to where Fred was sitting at one of the tables in the cafeteria area. She was just staring out the window at nothing.

Cotton crossed the room and took the seat across from her. "How about you?" he asked. "Are you okay?"

Fred's eyes suddenly jumped to Cotton, as if she had just been woken from a trance.

"No," she said. "How could I be?"

"You know that man had it coming," Cotton said. "What you did."

"Don't we all?" Fred asked.

"Depends on who you ask. Either way, I owe you one. But what happened to the gun I handed you? The Russian's?"

"I— I dropped it when the shooting started," Fred explained, clearly embarrassed. "That's why I used yours."

"It happens," Cotton replied. "But either way you can't let this get into your head. We need you."

"Why?" Fred asked.

"Because you have a trigger finger."

"Seriously?"

"Yes," Cotton said. "We're down from nearly a hundred fighters to *five*. By all accounts, we've got the Russian Army inbound and we're surrounded by a horde of black-eyed cannibals with superhuman speed and strength. If we're going to get through that and I'm going to find my daughter, we need every gun we can get—including yours."

"And if we get through all that?" Fred asked. "What then?"

"People never used to ask that question because the answer was that you get to live. Now folks don't have the Internet anymore or their fucking thousand-dollar phone and they think death is a good alternative. Civilization ruined us, but as near as I can tell, that's not much of a problem anymore. You're fighting for your life. You're fighting for your own survival, but more importantly, the survival of the man or woman beside you. So start damn acting like it."

"Okay," Fred said quickly. "I get it."

"Do you? Do you *really*?" Cotton asked, his steel blue eyes boring a hole through her.

"I do," Fred affirmed. "I didn't before, but I do now."

"Good."

Fred seemed as though something was on her mind. She hesitated for a moment and then went on. "I know it was my fault," she said.

"What was?" Cotton asked.

"Your daughter is missing. I know you came in here to find me."

"It's not your fault," Cotton said. "If it's anyone's fault, it's the men who took both you and April."

"I know you're right," Fred said. "It's just kind of hard to accept. For myself."

"Do you really have them?" Cotton asked. "The codes for the nukes?"

"I wish I didn't, but I do. Not the codes themselves—I doubt anyone has those anymore—but I helped design the command infrastructure. If I was able to plug directly into any facility system, I would most likely be able to gain control of the entire arsenal."

"Did Roland know that?"

Fred nodded. "Right from the very beginning," she said. "That's why I did all that work for him, fixing weapons and gear. I can fix anything, you know; it's just this thing I've got. So, I was able to help him, and he helped me by keeping me safe. I never really thought anyone was going to come after me and try to get what's inside my head, but I also never forgot how dangerous that information really was."

"So, Roland kept you safe to keep that information from falling into the wrong hands."

Fred turned to look at where Roland and Jorge were standing beside the main doors, calling to Harris to come in.

"I don't think that's why he did it," Fred said. "I think he did it so that, one day, he would be the one in control of that information."

Jean Wiley moved quickly through the woods and routinely glanced over her shoulder to make sure April was still within sight. The woman was limping badly, but she seemed able to keep pace.

Jean had snatched her pack up from where she and Cotton had left their gear just inside the tree line, and the weight slowed her down enough that April was mostly able to keep up. She'd thought about trying to take some of her father's things as well, but she wasn't sure if there might be more soldiers behind them. The best move was to just get out.

Finally, the thick brush ended, and Jean emerged onto the shoulder of a main road. She wasn't sure which road it was, but there didn't seem to be anyone around. She took a knee beside a tree and held up a hand for April to stop. The woman complied and waited under cover.

Jean looked down the length of road and scanned for any movement. Texas was a tactical double-edged sword. Because so much of it was flat—aside from the hill country—you could see people coming from an awful long way away, but that also meant they could see *you*. She thought back to the SLLS acronym her father had taught her.

Stop. Be present. Absorb your environment.

Look. What do you see? Is anything out of place? Are there any visible threats?

Listen. Do you hear a car engine in the distance coming toward you, people talking, other noises that don't belong?

Smell. Men smell a certain way, particularly if they haven't been in the field long.

Nothing. They were alone. She was sure of it.

Jean turned and waved April toward her. The woman limped forward and exited the woods onto the shoulder of the road.

Jean looked down at her wrapped leg. "How is it?" she asked.

"I feel it," April said, "but it doesn't feel like I think it should."

"Cannibals have a much higher pain tolerance than normal folks. That's probably why you aren't hurting a lot more. You'll also heal fast," Jean said as she stood up. "Cannibals do that, too. We'll check it once we're reasonably safe. I've got a full med-kit."

"Aren't we going back?" April asked.

"Where?"

"To the rail yard. Where Cotton is."

"No," Jean said. "We don't know what's happening there right now. We could be walking right into a fight we can't win."

April looked around and then back to Jean. "I don't hear any gunfire."

"That just means somebody won, but we don't know who. No, we're moving on. We'll link up with him down the road."

Jean walked onto the road and began heading for a truck she saw in the distance.

"Link up with him where?" April asked.

"Oatmeal," Jean said matter-of-factly. "Makes the most sense. That's where everyone was heading before, and it's a safe bet they'll keep heading in that direction. And they'll expect us to do the same."

"What if he goes into the woods to find you?" April asked.

"Got a fix for that," Jean said as she approached the truck.

The girl dropped her pack, reached in, and pulled out a thick piece of chalk from a ziplock bag. April watched as Jean spent the next several minutes drawing on the concrete until she finally stood up and wiped her brow, admiring her work.

"That's the Quaker Oatmeal man," April commented.

"That's right."

"That's weirdly good," April said.

She was right. It was a perfect reproduction of the man from the Quaker Oatmeal can.

"I was an artist," Jean said. "Before. Not the best, but not the worst either. Mostly line drawing, but some watercolors, too."

"Do you think you might be again someday?" April asked. "An artist, I mean."

"Nah," Jean said as she opened the driver's side door of the abandoned truck and slid onto the bench seat. She opened the glove box, fished out an old flathead screwdriver, and used it to pry open the steering column and expose the ignition wires. "World ain't got much need for artists anymore, in case that fact didn't capture your attention."

Jean used her multi-tool to strip some wires and spark the engine to life. She sat up and gestured for April to get in. The injured woman complied and got into the passenger seat.

"Where'd you learn to do that?" April asked.

"SEALs can do a lot of things normal folks can't. Like hotwire cars. You grow up around them and you learn how, too. One of Daddy's friends used to give me five dollars if I could hotwire a car in under a minute."

"And did you?"

"Like taking candy from a baby," Jean said with a smile.

Colonel Lebedev walked through the house and stopped. He looked back outside to where they had landed the transport helo in an open field. The rest of his Alpha Group men were searching the grounds and the surrounding area, all the way out to the main road. Of course they were looking for any available intelligence, but they were also attempting to calculate the death toll.

"What the hell happened here?" he asked himself as he stood in the living room, staring through the burned-out section of wall.

Lebedev looked down at the floor and, more specifically, the dozens of bodies covering it, like a blanket of the dead. From the rear door, Warrant Officer Balakin, his assistant team leader, entered with the same dismayed look on his face. Both men were veterans of endless military campaigns and had thought they'd seen all there was to see, but this was different.

The colonel took a knee and tapped the chest of one of the dead men. "Most of them are wearing plates."

"And they're all dressed the same, with shaved heads," Balakin replied. "And the crosses."

Lebedev looked back to the body and nodded. They had crosses carved into their foreheads.

"Some religious cult?" Balakin asked.

"I imagine," Lebedev answered and then smiled.

"But it looks like they ran into some people who did not want to be converted."

Balakin chuckled and turned as the Comms Sergeant walked up to the side of the house.

"Any contact?" Balakin asked.

"Negative," the Comms Sergeant replied.

Lebedev looked up to the overcast sky. "Atmospherics," he mused.

The Sergeant seemed as though something were on his mind, and Balakin noticed it. "What is it?" the Warrant Officer asked.

"It doesn't feel like the usual atmospheric interference," the Sergeant replied. "With that, I'd still get some static, maybe some broken transmission."

"And now?" Lebedev asked.

"It's like ... they're not there anymore."

Colonel Lebedev looked to Balakin and then back to the Sergeant. "How is that possible?"

"I don't know," the Sergeant replied.

The anomaly meant something, and Lebedev knew it could be significant. He had seen this man establish communications in some of the harshest environments known to man and under withering fire in the worst possible circumstances. He was nothing short of a wizard with even the most rudimentary communications gear.

"Okay," Lebedev said. "Tell the men to bring it in and begin prepping for extraction."

"To Marble Falls?" Balakin asked.

"Yes," Lebedev replied and then motioned to the Sergeant to leave. He waited for the man to be out of earshot and then turned to his second-in-command. "I have a bad feeling about this."

The statement caught Balakin's attention. He knew Colonel Lebedev to be a man with ice water in his veins, almost impervious to fear or trepidation.

"What do you think is happening?" Balakin asked.

Lebedev shook his head. "I cannot say, but as always, we must comply with our last order, which is to check in with Zhukov and his Polish troops at the Marble Falls rail yard. After we are finished there, we will head back to the Division and find out what has happened."

Sheila stood in the main room of the second story of Roland Reese's well-appointed house in the town of Oatmeal. She had managed to fight her way through the streets purely based upon having taken the slower-moving Gen 2 black-eyed cannibals by surprise.

Fortunately, it had been a short trip in a relatively straight line to Roland's house. Granted, she'd had to stop and put nearly a full magazine of AR rounds through the three locks on the main door, but she had made it.

The decision to head for Roland's place had been an easy one. Sheila knew that it was set up for a scenario exactly like this. He had a stock of food and water, weapons and ammunition, and comms gear. The second floor was also set up to be a strongpoint, complete with a steel door that dropped down onto the only opening from the bottom floor. In theory, she could hold out here for months.

However, as she stood at the second-floor window and looked down at the scores of black-eyed cannibals below, Sheila considered it a distinct possibility that even months might not be enough. The demons were all just standing there, silently staring up at her. She also knew they were in the house on the first floor, but the creatures had been unable to get past the steel door locking her in.

That in itself was an important point. *She* was the one cornered, not them, and it was only a matter of time before they would either find a way in or she would need to get out.

Sheila turned from the window and crossed the

main room to a large walk-in closet that had been transformed into a comms station. She sat down at the old wooden desk and tapped the sat-phone that lay atop its worn surface. The damn thing might as well have been a brick for all the good it had done her so far. None of the other numbers in the call directory were picking up.

She reached out and adjusted the settings on the HAM radio, then hit the scan button and put on the headphones. She had already tried this once but hadn't picked up much of anything. The reality was, there just weren't that many people within range who had decent communications equipment or even knew how to use it.

The static continued as the scan went on, and Sheila considered that she may just have to fight her way through the crowd outside and make a break for it. She knew where the motor pool was, and it wouldn't be hard to make it there and get a vehicle. She could easily outrun the Gen 2 cannibals, just as she had done to get to the house. She knew that she had a chance if she just did the proper planning.

Then a voice broke through the static, and Sheila's eyes snapped to the frequency on the display. She grabbed a Post-it note and wrote it down, then she realized what she was hearing.

The comms were Russian.

She knew these setups sometimes picked up stations from other countries. Was it possible she was picking up Russia?

Then she thought about the rumors that the Russians were in Canada, potentially getting ready to launch an invasion into the continental United States. Was that it? Was she picking up the Russian invasion force in Canada? A hell of a lot of good that would do her.

Sheila reached out for the microphone. She hesitated and then hit the call button. "Who is this?" she asked.

The voice stopped. It had sounded almost panicked.

"*American?*" the voice asked tentatively.

Sheila wasn't sure how much she should say, but really, how much more trouble could she get into?

"Yes," she replied.

"*Where are you?*" the voice inquired.

She had been right. It was panic in his voice.

"I'm not telling you that," Sheila said. "Where are you?"

There was a scraping sound on the radio, and the man came back much quieter. "*I think they know I'm here.*"

"Who? Where?"

"*We heard the stories,*" the voice said. "*About the cannibals. But they were wrong. They don't have white eyes.*"

"They have black eyes," Sheila said.

"*Everyone is dead,*" the voice continued. "*I'm the last one left. I'm trying to get out. Can you send help?*"

"Where are you?" Shiela insisted.

"*On Seventy-One. Near a town called La Grange.*"

Sheila felt her breath leave her. "That's in Texas," she said.

"*Yes,*" the voice replied. "*We were an entire division, but they chewed through us like we were nothing. It was over in an hour.*"

"Where are the rest of you?" Sheila asked. "Where is the rest of the Russian Army?"

"*If I tell you, will you come for me? Will you help me?*"

"Yes. Tell me where they are, and we'll send a rescue force."

"*Mostly in southern Oklahoma and New Mexico,*" the voice replied. "*But some divisions are already in Texas. When will you come?*"

"Soon," Sheila replied. "Just sit tight."

She reached forward and turned the radio off.

"It's a straight shot," April said as she read the map spread out on the dashboard while Jean drove. "Just keep going north on two eighty-one and then we'll hit twenty-nine at Burnet. From there, it's south to Oatmeal."

"Sounds like a plan," Jean replied as she scanned the road.

April folded the map and stuffed it into her pocket. She winced a bit as she shifted in her seat.

"Hurts?" Jean asked.

"A little bit," April said, "but I can take it."

"I've got some stuff in my pack," Jean said. "Oxy."

April's eyes went wide. "You have oxycontin?" she blurted.

"Not for fun, dummy." Jean laughed. "It's for things like this. Got antibiotics and other meds, too. If the pain gets bad enough that you need it, don't be shy about taking it."

"I'll hold off for now," April replied. "Need to keep my head clear."

"Suit yourself," Jean said and then leaned

forward over the steering wheel as much as she could. "Hold on."

Jean jerked the wheel to the left and took them off the road and into the trees, where she narrowly avoided hitting a tree trunk before slamming on the brakes. April slid forward and hit the dashboard, then let out a howl of pain.

Jean paid no mind as she dipped into her pack and then bailed out of the vehicle with a pair of binoculars and her MK18.

"What's happening?" April shouted.

"Stay in the truck!" Jean called back as she ran through the trees and took a knee a dozen feet from the road.

Ignoring her completely, April stepped out of the truck with her own rifle. Every step caused searing pain, but she pushed through it. Whatever was going on, it was important enough to nearly wreck their only mode of transportation, and now Jean was staring intently into the binos.

Then April saw what she was looking at.

"Is that a helicopter?" she asked, trying to see it clearly despite the sun in her eyes.

"Yes," Jean replied. "But it's not one of ours."

"How can you tell?"

"Same way I know most things," Jean said. "You

spend enough time on military bases watching helos fly around, you know what we've got and what we don't."

"Whose is it?"

Jean took the binos from her eyes and thought about it for a moment. "Can't say for sure," she replied. "But dollars to donuts, it's either the Russians or the Chinese. Maybe doing some deep recon."

April followed the helo as it moved overhead. "Almost looks like they're heading for the rail yard."

"Think you're right," Jean replied. "We need to get to Oatmeal and make sure Daddy and the others know about this."

Cotton had retrieved his pack from the woods, and sure enough, he'd found that Jean's things were gone. He was sure Jorge was right and that she was moving on to Oatmeal, as the most logical next stop for all of them. All the same, he'd stood there for several minutes looking and listening, but there was nothing.

Harris was still shell-shocked by Randall Eisler's death and everyone could see it, but all the same, he was going through the motions and staying on task. Despite Jorge's admission that he had sent Harris on a bit of a wild goose chase to keep him busy, the man had actually found a few useful pieces of information relating to U.N. connections to the Russian invasion force.

The more Cotton thought about it, it was so surreal that an *invasion* was actually happening. But, hell, according to everything he'd heard from Wik and now this latest conflict at the rail yard, it had already happened.

The possibility was something they'd always discussed in the Teams; the ultimate throw-down with the Russians. It was something everyone fantasized about, but no one actually wanted.

"Maybe you should talk to Harris," Cotton said to Fred, who was standing by the truck as they loaded it.

"Me?" Fred asked with surprise. "About what?"

"We're just gonna tell him to suck it up and carry on," Cotton said with a shrug. "I don't know. It might help to have a woman's ... perspective, I guess."

Fred understood. These men were long on gunfighting skills but short on bedside manner. As much as Harris had adapted to the new world, he didn't have the same background Cotton, Jorge, and Roland did. He wasn't accustomed to seeing his friends die. In fact, up until recently, he had never lost a single man. Now, he had lost all of them, and he'd watched Randall Eisler die right before his eyes.

Fred walked around to the rear of the truck, where Harris was loading a few water cans they had found and filled up. She studied him for a moment. He definitely wasn't right; his eyes were bouncing around as if they couldn't focus.

"Are you okay?" she asked.

Harris stopped what he was doing and looked at her. "I'm fine," he said.

Fred looked at the ground for a moment. "I had to kill my friend this morning."

Harris stopped what he was doing and looked at her.

"Her name was Celeste," Fred went on. "I say she was my friend, but really she was more like a daughter to me. She kind of ... I don't know. She was a little flighty, but she was a young girl. Only twenty-two."

"What happened?" Harris asked. "If you don't mind saying."

"She took the Gen 2 vaccine. The last time I saw her, she was walking into the woods with the other recipients, singing camping songs, going on a "vision quest," as they called it. You know, they had a different viewpoint on this whole thing. They were trying to will it to be something other than it was; something positive. I knew it was foolish, but it also seemed to be going okay for them, so who was I to try and take away their hope?"

Fred paused but said nothing.

"She turned?" Harris asked. "Didn't she?"

There were tears forming in Fred's eyes, but she did her best to hold them back. "I had to do it," she said. It sounded more like she was trying to convince herself than Harris. "Right?"

Harris nodded. "You didn't have a choice."

"I'm really bad at consoling people," Fred said with a nervous laugh. "But maybe you get my point?"

"Of course," Harris lied.

"We've got one piece of business to attend to before we head out," Roland said once they'd finished prepping the two trucks they would take back to Oatmeal. "Something we can't ignore."

"What's that?" Cotton asked.

"It's chow time," Roland said with a smile.

"It can't wait?" Cotton followed up.

"Maybe," Roland said. "But we don't know what we're about to walk into. Don't want to get in a bad spot where we're fighting and start going down with hunger pains."

"He's right," Jorge said.

"Fine," Cotton said. "I get it."

"There's one in that railcar," Harris said, nodding to one of the boxcars across the yard.

Cotton's confusion was obvious.

"They're everywhere," he said, indicating the bodies that littered the yard.

Then he understood. There was a look on Jorge and Fred's faces bordering on shame.

"Alive," Cotton said, the realization hitting him. "There's a live one in that railcar."

"You must know how this works," Roland said. "Every minute that passes, the meat turns. Why do you think Gatherers always look so malnourished? Once the breathing stops and the blood ain't flowing, nutrient levels drop like a rock. You want strong fighters, you need to feed them a certain fuel."

"Can't let you do that," Cotton said, his posture changing.

"Come on, now," Jorge said. "You know I don't like this shit, but it is what it is. This ain't a train worth trying to stand in front of."

"You're really going to stand there and try to tell

me that an hour or so of someone being dead changes things that much?"

"How many people have you eaten?" Jorge snapped.

Cotton said nothing.

"That's what I thought," Jorge persisted. "I don't like doing this any more than you like hearing about it, but it has to be done."

Cotton heard a few truncated screams after the four had entered the railcar, then nothing more. The craziest part about it all wasn't that they were almost certainly eating the man alive; the craziest part was that they were the good guys.

The bad guys were out there speaking Russian and rolling tanks across the Midwest on a collision course with the Texas Meat Belt. The bad guys were the black-eyed cannibals being led by some woman who had an agenda still unknown.

This made Cotton think of something else. By all accounts, the scientists in the City States had been working on the Gen 2 vaccine for nearly a year, and this was the result. A collaboration of the best minds available and, most likely, unlimited funds had yielded a vaccine that not only did not reverse the effects of the first one, but it upgraded existing cannibals into a hyper-charged version of themselves.

Was that really an accident? It wasn't a line of thought Cotton was happy about pursuing, because if it wasn't an accident, then it meant all this could be part of some greater agenda.

Cotton looked up as motion caught his eye, and he saw the four exiting the darkness of the railcar. There was blood on their faces and hands.

"Okay," Roland said. "Let's not dawdle. We've got a date with destiny."

CHAPTER 9

Sheila stood at the window and watched the black-eyed cannibals wandering around the house. She had taken to referring to them as the 'Wasted.' She wasn't sure why, but it seemed like they were toothpaste tubes with some of the toothpaste squeezed out. They weren't as fast as the original black-eyed cannibals and she'd noticed they also seemed a little mentally slow, like they had brain fog or something.

At first, the horde had just been standing around the house, staring, not doing much of anything. Then some of them started to break from the crowd and moved down the street away from the house. At first, Sheila thought it was a good sign; that maybe they were leaving.

At least, until they started coming back with ladders.

"You have *got* to be shitting me," Sheila exclaimed as she watched the first one lean a ladder up against the side of the house.

She reached out the window with her right arm and tried to push the ladder away, but it was too tall and heavy. The Wasted were also walking around to the other side of the building. There were other windows on the second floor that they could access with the tall ladders.

Apparently, Roland hadn't thought it was important to defend the second floor from a ladder attack.

"Fine," Sheila said. "Have it your way."

She brought the AR up to her shoulder, aimed at the cannibals starting to climb the ladder, and began taking well-aimed shots. It wasn't hard to hit her marks, but then she heard two other loud *clank*s on the other side of the house. She couldn't possibly defend all three entry points.

Sheila moved quickly across the room and locked the two doors that led into the adjacent hallways. She then shoved a couch across the floor to block one of the doors. There was nothing substantial to block the other one, so firepower would have to do the job.

She looked back out the window and saw the

Wasted starting to come up the ladder. She fired a series of rounds down into them as they ascended. She wasn't getting headshots, but it was enough to slow them down.

The pack on the main desk caught her attention. She had grabbed it on her way out of the armory. Now, she unzipped it and pulled out two sticks of C4 and the corresponding remote detonators.

Sheila stared at them for a moment and then had a horrible realization: she had no idea which detonator went to which stick.

"*Shit!*" she screamed.

There was a rattling beside the window. Sheila looked up and then brought the barrel of the AR up to match. Two trigger pulls knocked back the cannibal that was trying come through the window.

Outside the two locked doors, she heard a commotion. The Wasted were already inside the hallway. Not only that, but it sounded like there were a lot of them.

Too many.

Colonel Lebedev looked down at the dead body of General Zhukov.

His death, culminating in the failure of the general's mission, was bad, and Lebedev knew it.

They were supposed to have been the Quick Reaction Force for Zhukov's mission. No one really cared about the supposed 'clean-up' mission to hunt down rebel cannibal forces leading up to the main invasion of the 'Texas Meat Belt' that everyone seemed so concerned about. No, Zhukov had an idea that there was something deeper going on in the American South, and that everything that had occurred wasn't an accident.

It was planned, and Zhukov wanted to find out who was behind it. To what end, Lebedev had no idea, but apparently the higher-ups thought it was important enough that they'd assigned an actual Alpha Group unit to be Zhukov's QRF, which was unheard of.

So, why hadn't the man called? Whatever had happened here was serious enough that it had laid waste to an entire unit of the Polish troops. Granted, they weren't exactly seasoned warfighters, but they also weren't pushovers. They should have put up at least some resistance. But during his quick assessment of the rail yard, Lebedev had seen that not all of the soldiers were there, and he was curious where the remainder might be.

And yet, there was only a single enemy body. A dead man lying beside one of the rail cars with a stab wound to his neck.

Lebedev walked to the small office that Zhukov had clearly set up shop in and looked around. There were papers scattered around, as if someone had been rifling through it, potentially looking for intelligence. He wondered if those responsible had found anything.

Then he saw it—or, more specifically, he *didn't* see it. He walked back out to the main room, knelt down beside Zhukov's body, and went through the dead man's pockets.

The small journal the general always kept with him was gone. Someone had taken it.

Balakin walked in and saw his commander kneeling beside Zhukov's body. Lebedev looked up.

"Anything?" the colonel asked.

"Not here," Balakin replied. "But the men in the helo just reported back from their recon up the road. There was some kind of a firefight in the main town, near a string of car dealerships."

"The rest of the unit?"

"I imagine so," Balakin said. "They're still in the air if you want them to touch down and do a ground assessment."

"No," Lebedev said as he stood up. "We have more pressing matters to attend to. General Zhukov always kept a journal with him, usually on his person."

"It's not there?" Balakin surmised.

"Nowhere to be found, and I suspect that what happened here is linked to whatever he found. And whatever *that* is, it's in that journal."

"So, what's our next move?"

Lebedev sighed. "Return to Divison. We'll make contact with Colonel Nikitin and attempt to source further intelligence."

Cotton watched the truck ahead of them and did another quick check of his gear. For the first time in a while, his head felt clear. He'd always been coherent enough to do what he needed to, but he'd also felt almost as if he were walking underwater, partially in a dream state. Things moved just a little more slowly than they should have, and he always felt that his eyes and his body were slightly disconnected.

Now, he felt as normal as he ever had. Perhaps it was being separated from Jean that had snapped everything into focus. He had noticed something similar when the Nephilim had taken her the other night. He had momentarily achieved the same level of clarity.

Cotton had opted to ride with Fred while Jorge, Roland, and Harris took the lead truck.

"Can I trust you?" Fred asked spontaneously.

"As much as you can anyone else, I imagine," Cotton replied.

"It's just ... you seem like you're one of the good guys."

"Maybe to my detriment."

Fred laughed. "You didn't have to come for me," she went on. "You didn't even have to come for April, but you did. Not only that, but you don't seem to be a big fan of cannibals. And still you came."

"I wasn't going to," Cotton replied. "So, maybe I'm not as good as you think."

"Why did you, then?"

"Jean," Cotton said. "She reminded me that maybe we're supposed to be good. Instead of just surviving. Maybe surviving ain't enough."

"I know more than I've said," Fred blurted.

Cotton turned to her. "Am I gonna wish I hadn't heard this?"

"Probably," Fred replied.

Cotton sighed. "Okay. Give it to me."

"When you do the kind of work I did for the

government, you get put on a list. It's a short one, and not many people have access to it, but the ones that do have deep pockets."

She hesitated.

"Go on," Cotton pressed.

"Three years ago, I was approached through a series of cutouts to do some statistical analysis on a theoretical depopulation event."

"*What?*" Cotton nearly shouted.

"People ask for stuff like that all the time!" Fred countered, clearly on the defensive. "It never usually turns into anything!"

"It's fine," Cotton said, calming himself. He knew that blowing his top would probably cause the woman to clam up, and if he wanted the truth, he needed to let her speak. "I didn't mean to react the way I did. Tell me what happened."

"The client wanted to know what would happen to the population based on three separate events. The first was a basic virus with relatively low mortality. They specifically wanted to know what the collateral fallout would be, i.e., impact on the economy, mental health, riots, etc., and how that would impact reduction of the population. The second event was a virus with high transmissibility that would cause people to kill each other. Basically, engineered psychosis."

"Or to become cannibals," Cotton surmised.

"Yeah," Fred said. "That's what I figured afterward. The second event was a fail-safe, in case the first didn't get the numbers down to where they wanted them to be. Of course, this was all veiled as being an estimate of what would happen in the wake of a 'terror attack.'"

"Right. They weren't coming right out and saying this was something they were actively planning." Cotton paused for a moment. "You said three events."

"The third event was something that wasn't supposed to happen. It would only be needed if ... well, if humanity found a way. If people found a way to survive the first two."

"What was the third event?"

"It's almost certainly an EMP," Fred said decidedly. "It makes the most sense. You would eliminate the population without harming the infrastructure. In the probability models we were building, an event like that dropped the Earth's population to two million."

"I'm sorry, I think I misheard you," Cotton

replied. "It sounded like you just said there would only be *two million* people left on the entire planet."

"The equivalent of a global extinction event. They would finally get what they want."

"Why the hell would *anyone* want that?" Cotton asked.

"There are theories," Fred said with a shrug. "Depopulating the planet in order to save it is the most plausible one."

"What?"

"In 1900, the world's population was one point six billion. Before all this happened, we were up to nearly eight billion. It doesn't take a mathematician to figure out that is unsustainable growth, but we were still doing it and we were shredding the planet in the process. There was always talk about this idea that Mother Nature would eventually drive a course correction and significantly drop the population. I think there may have been some people who thought she needed a little help to speed up the process."

"Kill everyone to save the planet?" Cotton asked. "That's the dumbest thing I've ever heard."

"So was killing the Jews to save the Fatherland," Fred said. "But it still happened."

"How do we stop it?" Cotton asked.

"I don't know," Fred said. "But I might know someone who does. If he's still alive."

"Who is it? Where is he?"

"He was a colleague of mine. Doctor Gregory Wilson. As to where he is, that's where things get problematic."

"Because they're going so smoothly up to now?"

"He's in Houston."

Cotton understood. "Surrounded by a million black-eyed cannibals."

"That's about the size of it," Fred affirmed.

Cotton looked ahead to see a sign indicating they were only five miles outside of Oatmeal.

"Okay," he said. "Let's focus on one disaster at a time."

Sheila pulled the AR tight to her body in order to free up her hand to position one stick of C4 near the window and stuff the second in her hip pocket. If she hit the wrong detonator switch, she would most likely never even know it had happened.

A switch mounted on the wall would trigger the steel door that had so far done a commendable job of separating her from the throngs of black-eyed cannibals that were no doubt swarming the first floor. To her right, Sheila could see the door to the hallway rattling on its hinges as the cannibals in the hallway battered it with their fists. She had to keep reminding herself they weren't like zombies; they had a thought process and would eventually figure out a way through that door, if they hadn't already.

The plan was simple, and she knew it would work because it had to. There was no other option. Just as long as she hit the right switch for the right stick of C4.

"Hello, God? Are you there?" she asked. "It's me again. Sheila. I know I'm new at this, but if you could lend a sister a hand here, I'd really appreciate it."

She caught the unintentional joke about her missing limb and smiled as she reached up to trigger the switch that would open the steel door.

Sheila let out a breath, then hit it.

The spring holding the steel door released, and it popped open much more quickly than she had anticipated.

"*Holy shit!*" she shouted.

There were easily thirty of the Wasted crowding the first floor, and within a second, they were racing up the stairs. Sheila stepped back, released the pull tab on her sling, brought the AR up, and performed a magazine dump into the stairwell. It worked; the suppressive fire caused the attacking cannibals to tumble down the stairs and onto the floor below.

She grabbed the stick of C4 from her pocket and hurled it into the midst of the crowd, then turned and dove to the floor, hitting the detonator switch as she did so.

The sound of the explosion was deafening, and Sheila could feel heat on her back and the floor rising beneath her. It had been purely a guess that the amount of explosive she'd decided on wouldn't completely flatten the house. She had been lucky, if you could call it that.

Everything was on fire and her ears were ringing again, much louder than before, as she stumbled to her feet. Without thinking, Sheila dropped the empty magazine from the AR, retrieved a fresh one from her cargo pocket, and slammed it into the magazine well, then sent the bolt forward, all with only one hand. From there, she descended the stairwell with her weapon up.

There were bodies and body parts everywhere, but not a single cannibal had survived. Blood splattered the walls amid the flames—or at least, what was left of them. It was like a scene out of hell.

There were still a handful of the Wasted wandering the street outside, clearly disoriented from the blast. Sheila knew she wouldn't get another opportunity like this, so she lined up her red dot and began taking slow, well-aimed headshots at the targets presented to her as she advanced out the front door.

Once she was clear of the house and in the street, she turned, fished the second detonator out of her pocket, and looked up. She could see dozens of the cannibals through the upstairs windows.

"You're fucking evicted," she hissed, and dropped the hammer on the second detonator.

The house imploded, the second story first seeming to expand slightly like a man who had eaten too much for dinner and then rapidly collapsing inward and falling directly onto the first floor.

Sheila felt the pressure wave hit her a split second before realizing she didn't have enough stand-off distance from the house. The next thing she felt was a hard impact against her back, and then she was momentarily unconscious as she rolled off the hood of the sedan and hit the street.

Car alarms were sounding all around her as Sheila realized she had been thrown backward into the windshield of a car. Looking across the street, she also observed that she had traveled about fifteen feet through the air to reach her destination.

Miraculously, the AR-15 was still secured to her as she stood up, but she could feel she had sustained yet another injury. Something in her back was seriously out of joint and caused her to limp as she began moving down the street.

Sheila saw them first in the reflection of a store window, coming up fast behind her. There weren't many of them, maybe just a couple dozen, but that number would still be enough to run her down. The motor pool was only a few blocks away, near the main gate, but she was beginning to feel a throbbing pain in her left hip that was seriously slowing her down.

It was time to use some strategy. She began leapfrogging from one car to the next, using the cover each provided to get off a few shots at the advancing horde. It seemed that for every three or four rounds she got off, she was getting at least one solid hit. With three more blocks and dozens of parked cars, she knew she had a chance at making it.

Assuming her body could carry her that far. She was bleeding from the stump of her left arm again, there were a dozen other significant cuts on her body, blood was streaming into her eyes, and she felt like she was breathing fire. Sheila knew that cannibals were stronger and tougher than normal folk, but there was a limit to that, and she felt like she was fast approaching that threshold.

Before she knew it, the entrance to the motor pool was coming up fast, only a few dozen feet away. Beyond that was the main entrance to the town.

Sheila could feel herself smiling through the blood and the sweat as her feet pounded the pavement toward the entrance to the motor pool. It was time. She was going to make it. She felt a giddiness rising inside of her.

Then the door swung open and the first of a half dozen black-eyed cannibals surged out of the building toward her.

"*No!*" she screamed as she brought the AR up and dumped what remained of her magazine into the would-be attackers.

It was enough to slow them down, and she pivoted again. She hit the quick disconnect on her sling and let the rifle clatter to the ground. That last salvo had been it; she was now out of ammunition. At this point, the only thing the weapon could do was slow her down.

Instinct took her toward the front gate, but she had no idea what good that would do her. She could feel the tears welling in her eyes as she sprinted forward.

She didn't even have a round left for herself.

"Shit," April said as she put a hand to her forehead. "I feel hot."

The wind whipping through the cabin of the truck should have been cooling her off, so Jean knew what the woman was implying: she was running a fever.

"How bad is it?" Jean asked.

"I don't know," April said as she tried to control her breathing. She knew that she had a habit of spiraling when things went south, and she needed to keep herself together. "I'll be fine. I just need to get this thing taken care of."

"How's the pain?"

"It's okay. It's just this dull throbbing. I can handle it."

Jean leaned forward in her seat and smiled as she saw the main entrance to the town of Oatmeal: two jack-knifed big rigs, forming what amounted to the front gate.

"They'll have more medicine here," Jean asserted. "Better than the stuff I've got."

April blinked her eyes a few times as she

surveyed the entrance and then shook her head. Something was wrong. She knew it.

"Why isn't there a guard?" she asked.

Then she saw her. The woman was a bloody mess, and as near as April could tell, one of her arms was missing. Her graying hair was flying everywhere as she sprinted toward them, still nearly one hundred feet away.

"What's she running from?" Jean asked and then quickly received her answer.

The black-eyed cannibals came pouring out of the gate behind her, at least twenty of them, maybe more.

"We can't fight them all!" April snapped.

"Buckle up," Jean said calmly, her West Virginia twang standing out in bold relief.

April complied, reaching for her seat belt without thinking about it. "What are you going to do?"

"What needs doin'," Jean replied as she slammed her foot down on the accelerator.

They were heading straight for Sheila when Jean yanked the wheel to the left, pointing the truck at the biggest cluster of cannibals behind the woman. The truck bucked slightly as it plowed into several of them, and then Jean slammed on the brakes, threw it in reverse, and traveled backwards several feet until she'd caught up with Sheila.

"Get in!" Jean shouted.

April leaned out the window with Jean's Glock 19 and fired several rounds as the black-eyed cannibals advanced on the truck.

Without hesitation, Sheila used her last ounce of strength to pull herself over the side of the truck and into the bed. She could feel her heart racing and her vision blurred as she finally let her muscles rest. In that moment, she stared up at the blue Texas sky and felt a strong calm wash over her.

By now, the cannibals had surrounded them, and April's rapid firing of the nine millimeter pistol was not doing much to dissuade them.

Jean put the truck back into drive, sped forward, turned around, and, as she came back upon the crowd, threw the vehicle into neutral. She tapped the brake and quarter-turned the steering wheel, throwing the truck into a one-eighty. The rear of the vehicle spun around like a giant hammer, slamming into the group of cannibals. One was hit particularly hard; the black-eyed cannibal was launched into the air and landed, inopportunely, in the back of the truck.

Without pause, the cannibal was clambering on

top of Sheila, and within a moment, every muscle in her body went from being relaxed to as taut as a trip wire. She spun her hips and threw the creature against the side of the truck bed. She felt something behind her with her right hand and grasped it. Without even knowing what it was, Sheila hurled it forward, and the pair of gardening shears plunged into the throat of the cannibal as it lunged for her.

"*Die! Die! Die!*" she screamed as she slammed him into the bed of the truck.

The truck lurched to a stop, and Jean knew what had happened. One of the wheels was stuck, grinding into the bodies of the dead. The remaining cannibals were advancing on the truck, some carrying sticks and clubs.

"Kill them all!" Jean shouted as she pushed herself back against the seat of the truck and brought the shorty MK18 up to the windshield.

Jean remembered from the fight at Cypress Mill that these black-eyed cannibals didn't go down easy, and shots to the heart or head were necessary if you wanted to turn them off like a switch. She also remembered her father saying that if you were shooting from inside of a vehicle, you needed to aim a few inches lower because the angle of the round would be deflected up by the angle of the glass. She wasn't one hundred percent sure whether that applied to ARs or just pistols, so she decided to split the difference and aim for the throat.

Jean unleashed her 5.56 rounds through the glass as April fired the Glock beside her. The cannibals didn't seem to have any fear and pushed through the withering gunfire, even reaching into the vehicle for them.

The truck was rocking as Jean reloaded the AR in the confined space and then watched with horror as another group of the black-eyed beasts streamed out from the front gate.

There were so many.

Too many.

Sheila slashed forward with the gardening shears as the cannibals tried to climb into the truck bed. She felt like she was starting to lose consciousness as she fought. She wasn't certain if it was from blood loss or just fatigue, but either way, it didn't matter. The lights were going out.

Then she looked up, and everything snapped into focus. They had stalled next to one of the big rigs at the front gate. She could jump from the back of the truck to the hood of the closest one. She knew she could. She had to.

"Please, God," she cried. "Help me."

Sheila took one more slash with the gardening shears, then dropped them, turned, stepped up onto the edge of the truck bed, and leapt for the side of the rolled semi.

She didn't think she was going to make it. She couldn't. It was too far.

But she did.

Sheila felt her hip crack against the steel of the truck and held on for dear life with her one hand. Slowly, she got her grip and began to climb forward. She felt a few hands brush against her legs, but she knew the beasts would have trouble getting up the side of the truck without jumping from the other vehicle as she had. She'd also observed that while the Wasted weren't quite 'zombies,' they did seem to have some issues with fine motor control. No doubt it would take them a while to follow her up to the top of the truck, but that was time they would not have.

. . .

Jean felt the bolt on her MK18 lock to the rear, and her chest tightened. That was it: she was out of ammo.

At almost the exact same moment, April's pistol went into slide lock. She, too, was out.

Jean spun in her seat and began delivering muzzle strikes at the cannibals reaching through her window. She felt hot breath on her face and teeth snapping beside her ear. Her hand dropped to the knife on her belt, she drew it, and she lashed out at the man who was trying to turn her into dinner.

"We have to get out of this *fucking truck!*" April screamed.

In one seamless moment, Jean felt the world fall away. Her heart rate slowed down, and her vision opened up from the tunnel it had been constrained to. She reached into her pocket and drew out the standard fifteen round Glock mag she kept there.

"Give me the gun," Jean said calmly and held out her hand.

The cannibals were smashing out the windshield in an effort to get inside. The only thing stopping them from crawling in through the windows was their own clumsy efforts, several of them trying to reach in at once. Jean felt fingers brush her hair, and she smiled. She was going to be with her mother again.

April passed the pistol to the young girl. She already knew what she was going to do.

Sheila clawed her way up the side of the trailer attached to the back of the semi. Once she was on the top, she collapsed and looked up again at that same Texas sky she had seen from the truck bed.

"Just a little more," she said quietly. "Just a little more."

She was beyond exhaustion. Her muscles pumped battery acid and she was breathing fire as she pulled herself to her feet and walked to the large tarp secured over an equally large object. She looked down at the crowd of cannibals swarming the truck. If those women inside were still alive, they wouldn't be for much longer. They had tried to save her; now, Sheila was going to return the favor.

She unhooked the bungees securing the tarp in place and then pulled it back to reveal the Browning M2 fifty caliber machine gun. She worked the charging handle and clutched one of the two grip handles with her right hand. She knew she was going to have a hell of a time keeping the weapon on target, but she also knew she was out of options.

Sheila had never fired the fifty cal before, but she'd seen the men working with it enough to understand the basic mechanics and what made it different from other machines guns, specifically the butterfly trigger mounted to the rear as opposed to being in a trigger guard forward of the lower receiver. Sheila shoved the stump of her left arm against the side of the other grip handle and swung the barrel toward the mob below.

There was no need to aim. At this distance, she couldn't miss.

Jean pushed the magazine with their only remaining rounds into the Glock 19 and worked the slide. She turned to April. She could feel hands grasping at her through the window, clawing at her face.

April parted her lips to speak.

"Don't say anything," Jean said curtly. "It'll only make this harder."

She pressed the barrel into the space between April's lips and nose. It would be a clean shot, turning her off like a light. The woman wouldn't even know it had happened.

Jean took up the slack on the trigger. This wasn't the hard part; the hard part would be turning the gun on herself after seeing what it did to April, but she would do it. She knew she would. She would pull the trigger a second time and find herself standing at that river the pastor always talked about in church. She would look across to the opposite shore and see everyone she had ever loved. She would see her mom again.

Jean felt her index finger hit the wall of the trigger and watched April close her eyes and clench her jaw.

Then it happened. The truck rocked, and Jean felt blood spray against her face. Then every window seemed to shatter simultaneously, and it felt as if thunder were rolling inside of her head.

Everything went black.

"*Yeah!*" Sheila screamed as the fifty caliber rounds impacted all around the truck, a few of them striking it as she struggled to maintain control of the heavy gun. "Suck on that, you sons of bitches!"

It was far from a perfect display of machine gunnery, but despite only having one and a half arms to work with, Sheila was managing to hit most of what she aimed at. The beauty of the fifty caliber rounds was that she didn't even need clean shots. Any hit to the body of one of the cannibals was enough to literally tear them apart, and the shock wave produced by the bullets hitting the ground around them was at least sufficient to topple them.

This was the first time Sheila saw the Wasted displaying anything approximating some sort of survival instinct. They began running. They were not fearless, not after all, but she wasn't going to let them get off that easily. A few made it around the corner of the second truck toward Main Street, so Sheila walked her fire directly through the body of the truck, the rounds more than powerful enough to pierce the truck and its engine block and destroy the fleeing cannibals on the other side.

By now, there were only a handful left standing, and they were fleeing down the main road away from Oatmeal and, more importantly, away from Sheila and her fifty caliber machine gun. Sheila released her grip on the gun and reached into one of her cargo pockets. She didn't even realize she was doing it until she had pulled the cigarette from its package and put it between her lips.

She watched the running black-eyed cannibals as she lit it and took a contemplative drag. She knew it was one hundred percent the wrong thing to be doing in the condition she was in, but that had also never stopped her before.

She reached back down and gripped the Browning's handle, then turned the gun on the runners.

"Only gonna die tired," she said as she hit the butterfly trigger.

The heavy rounds ripped through the air and impacted short of the runners, but it only took a moment for Sheila to adjust her fire and watch the impacting rounds tear the fleeing cannibals to shreds.

As if on cue, the belt-fed machine gun ran dry. Smoke was coming from the feed tray, and she could feel the heat emanating from the barrel. Sheila bent over and picked up the cigarette that had fallen from her mouth while she was running the fifty cal. It had gone out, so she pressed it to the red hot barrel and it smoldered back to life.

There were bodies and dismembered limbs everywhere, and the earth was soaked through with blood.

Jean could feel the water on her legs. It felt real. It *was* real. She was standing in the river, in that same one the preacher always talked about, the one where she would see everyone she ever loved on the other side.

Sure enough, there they all were on the opposite shore. She saw her grandparents, even though her daddy's father had passed away a long time ago, back when Jean was still little.

She hadn't known her grandmother had passed, but she had imagined as much after the last time Daddy had picked her up from Grandma's house. Jean knew from the way they were talking that she would never see her grandmother again. Yet, there she was, over on that opposite shore.

Then Jean felt a warmth on her face, and she broke into the biggest, broadest smile ever.

Momma was there. She was wearing a white gown, and her hair was done up like something out of the movies. She walked forward into the water and met Jean. Jean moved forward to throw her arms around her, but her momma stopped her.

"You can't be here," Momma said. "Not yet."

"I ... I want to," Jean said. "I want to be here. I want to be with you."

"You always were a daddy's girl," Sarah Wiley said with a smile. "You know that?"

Jean looked around.

"Where is he?" Jean asked. "I thought he'd be

here. Isn't that how it works? We all end up in the same place together? Don't matter when we die, we all answer the call the same?"

Sarah reached out and touched her daughter's face. Her hand was trembling. "I'm so sorry," she said, her voice wavering. "I never wanted this for you, not any of this. It wasn't supposed to be like this."

Sarah hesitated and looked over her shoulder, back to the shore she had come from. Her own mother was there, Jean's grandmother. The older woman simply shook her head, and Sarah turned back to her daughter.

"We will be together again someday, my love. It just can't be now," Sarah said. "You have to go back."

Sarah Wiley placed her hand on her young daughter's head and pushed her under the water.

CHAPTER 10

"Come on!" Sheila shouted as she slapped Jean across the face. "Wake the hell up!"

"That's not helping!" April snapped as she rifled through Jean's pack. It had taken her a moment to find the rucksack from where it had become wedged when the truck flipped over. "She doesn't have a heartbeat!"

"I'm sorry!" Sheila said as she sat back on her knees and looked down at the girl. "I need her to be okay!"

"I need you to calm down," April said, trying to steady her own voice as well. Finally, her hand found what she was looking for, and she pulled it from the medical kit in the pack. "If we're going to help her, we have to stay calm."

April had already tried all of the standard life-saving steps, but nothing had worked. There was no respiration; no heartbeat; no nothing. She couldn't know for sure without the benefit of a full examination, but April's best guess was that the repeated concussive effect of the fifty caliber rounds ripping through the truck combined with Jean's high sympathetic nervous system tone had stopped the girl's heart.

April looked at the adrenaline shot and then back to Jean. "Shit," she said. "Okay, we're going to do this."

"What's wrong?" Sheila asked, sensing that April wasn't sure about the decision.

"This stuff can cause brain damage," April said. "But we're out of options. Hold her still. She might be moving pretty fast when she wakes up. *If* she wakes up."

Jean didn't know which way was up. After her mother had pushed her under the water, there were brief flashes of sunlight for a moment, but then only darkness. Now, she was tumbling in the dark water, trying to find her bearings and becoming rapidly aware that she needed to breathe but couldn't.

Was this really how it ended? In the darkness, unable to escape, waiting until she was finally forced to pull that dark water into her lungs?

Then she saw a sliver of light. It was coming from her left, but was that really up? Jean didn't get caught up in this strange internal debate. Instead she turned her body and kicked with everything she had left. Her muscles were burning, and she knew she was running out of oxygen. She didn't have much time.

As she kicked and expended what little energy her body had left, the light became brighter. Then she felt a pull; a steady tug reminiscent of a current pulling her into the light. She moved closer and closer to the light source and finally reached out her hand to it, grasping at the light.

She felt a hard pull on her hand, and then the light enveloped her.

Jean opened her mouth and sucked in a full breath of air. Her eyes were wide, her pupils the size of saucers, and her breathing immediately ramped up.

"Let her go!" April shouted.

Sheila complied, and Jean instantly rolled over

and vomited on the ground. April held the girl's hair back as she retched.

"It's okay," April said. "You're okay. This is normal. I hit you with the adrenaline from your pack."

"I ..." Jean said with labored breathing. "I was saving that for an emergency."

April laughed out loud. "I think this qualifies," she said. "Now I need you to stand up. You've got a nasty scratch on your shoulder."

"I do?" Jean asked as she worked her way to standing, her balance obviously impaired from the aftereffects of the dose of adrenaline.

"Here, I'll check," April said, and she took Jean's left arm in what looked like a jiu-jitsu hold. She quickly jerked Jean's arm, and it went back into place with a loud *pop*.

Jean screamed, mostly in surprise. "What the hell was that?"

"Your shoulder was dislocated," April explained. "Easiest way to get it back in is for you not to know it's about to happen."

Jean frowned and rubbed her shoulder, but nodded her understanding all the same.

April looked Sheila over. "You look messed up,"

she said, studying the stump of Sheila's left arm. "I assume that wasn't like that yesterday?"

Sheila had turned to look at the town, and April realized she couldn't hear her. She tapped Sheila on the arm, and the woman turned to her.

"Did you lose your hearing?" April asked.

Sheila nodded. "Earlier," she said. "Maybe a few times. I think I'm mostly reading lips."

"Okay," April said. "Is there an infirmary in the town? We need to get you cleaned up."

Jean looked off in the distance and saw vehicles heading toward them. "You've *got* to be kidding me," she said.

"Maybe it's your father," April reasoned.

"And maybe it ain't," Jean replied as she walked to the wreckage of the truck. She knew they didn't have a single round left between the three of them as the Glock was hopelessly lost in the twisted wreckage.

She reached in the broken window, retrieved her knife, and rejoined April and Sheila.

Cotton leaned forward in the passenger seat of the truck he was sharing with Fred, and his eyes widened.

"Floor it!" he shouted.

Fred obeyed without thinking and slammed the accelerator down with her foot. They quickly overtook the lead truck being driven by Roland, Jorge, and Harris and whipped around them as they advanced on Oatmeal.

Jean tightened her grip on the knife, but she didn't waver from her position as she watched the rear truck speed past the forward one.

She had come this far over the past year, and she wasn't about to back down now. Whoever this was, if they weren't friendly, they were about to be in for the fight of their lives.

Fred stopped the truck about fifty feet from the three women, and Cotton was out the door before the vehicle finished moving. He didn't even grab his AR. Instead, he sprinted forward and picked his little girl up in his arms.

"Baby Bear!" he shouted as he hugged his daughter.

The knife fell from Jean's hand, and she allowed herself to relax. She wrapped her arms around her father but still held back the tears that wanted to come. He held her tighter.

"*Ow!*" she called out.

Cotton set her down. "What's wrong?"

"She dislocated her shoulder," April explained.

"And had a heart attack," Sheila offered.

"We could have saved that for later," April countered.

"*Heart attack?*" Cotton blurted. "What the hell happened here?"

Then he saw it for the first time: the aftermath of the fight the women had been in with the black-eyed cannibals. His vision had been so focused on his daughter that he had barely noticed the scores of dead bodies and the fifty caliber holes that riddled nearly everything in sight.

"Got in a fight, is all," Jean answered. "And they're the worse for it."

Cotton looked into his daughter's eyes. They were cold; colder than they had been even that morning. So much had happened since then.

"What the hell happened here?" Roland called out as he exited the truck.

"*I* fucking happened," Sheila responded. "No thanks to you." She still couldn't hear much of anything, but she'd been able to read Roland's lips and the expression on his face.

Jorge felt his heart drop when he saw Sheila. Just yesterday, she had been as vibrant as the day he met her. Now, she was changed, and it was more than just the physical damage. He ran to her and attempted to reach out, but Sheila recoiled.

Which was when he finally noticed her left arm was missing below the elbow.

"My God," Jorge gasped. "Your ... Your—"

"I ate my arm," Sheila snapped. "And if it's all the same to you, I'd rather not talk about it."

"Hey, listen up!" April shouted. "We don't have time for old home week. I've got a bone sticking out of my leg that's not going to put itself back in, and these two need medical attention, right now."

Cotton stood against the wall of Oatmeal's infirmary with Jorge and Roland. They watched as April finished stitching up a particularly nasty cut Jean had sustained to her left arm, most likely from shrapnel unleashed by Sheila's machine gun show. April had been insistent that she needed to attend to Sheila first, who was clearly much worse off than Jean, but the woman had refused.

Sheila was a woman who hadn't received much help from anyone in her life, and the realization that Jean had risked her life to save her, a total stranger, had set her back on her heels.

"She's bleeding out of her fucking ears," Jorge said quietly as he watched Sheila.

Roland turned and looked his old friend in the eyes. "Hey, *hermano*, she'll be fine. She's tough, right? Even tougher than she was before you left, and that was pretty damn tough." Roland couldn't help but smile. "Hell, she flattened half the town and took on a horde of those things with a freakin' fifty cal—and all with one arm."

Jorge tried to smile. "Yeah, I know you're right. It's just hard seeing her like this."

"Look, I know you don't want to hear this, but you have to be ready for the possibility that nothing has changed," Roland said, his voice becoming serious. "Between you two."

"I know," Jorge said with a nod.

Roland put his hand on Jorge's shoulder for a moment but said nothing. He turned to Cotton. "We need to do a sweep of the town. You up for it?"

"Can do," Cotton replied.

"I can do it," Jorge said.

"You sure?" Roland asked.

"Yeah, I'm fine."

"Take Harris, then."

***

"You coming?" Jorge asked as he exited the building and found Harris in the parking lot.

Harris looked shaken and a little zoned out. He'd looked that way ever since Randall Eisler had died at the rail yard, and Jorge had a strong suspicion the former marauder leader thought it was his fault.

"Where to?" Harris asked, snapping out of his stupor.

"Clearing the town," Jorge replied as he slipped his arm into his sling and secured the recce rifle to his body. He also tapped his pistol in its holster and did a quick magazine check. "Not expecting to find much of anything, but keep your head on a swivel. You never know."

"Roger that," Harris replied, and without realizing it, he copied Jorge's movements, securing his rifle and checking his gear.

The two men walked down the side of the street toward the eastern edge of Oatmeal. Jorge made sure to check his surroundings, but he was mostly going through the motions. He didn't expect to actually find anything.

"How you feeling?" he asked.

Harris responded with surprise on his face. "What do you mean?"

"You think it was your fault, don't you?" Jorge ventured.

Harris stopped in his tracks. "Do *you* think it was?"

Jorge stopped and turned to face the much shorter man. "Yes," he replied coldly.

The answer clearly surprised Harris.

"It was your job to watch his six," Jorge went on. "You weren't doing that—you were doing some other fucking thing—and Randall Eisler paid the ultimate price."

Harris parted his lips but then stopped himself from saying what he was about to. He was about to make an excuse, but he knew that it was wrong.

"You're right," he said eventually. "I fucked up."

"That's what you're supposed to do," Jorge said.

"What?" Harris asked, confused.

"You see it a lot, especially on the flat range. Guys want to be perfect. They want to be 'that guy,' the one who never makes a mistake; never gets chastised. Thing is, those guys never end up being 'that guy.' They're just stagnant. They never get better. Yeah, you fucked up, and yeah, this time the price was pretty damn high. A man died because of it. But you honor him by learning from that mistake and getting better, not by walking around feelin' sorry for yourself."

Harris knew the big man was right. "I understand."

"I know you understand," Jorge said, "but do you get it?"

"I get it," Harris said without hesitation.

"I thought you were a fucking joke when I met you," Jorge said impassively. "Prove me wrong."

"Remind you of the old days?" Roland asked as he walked with Cotton toward the western edge of Oatmeal.

"You weren't a cannibal then," Cotton replied and then caught himself. He stopped and turned to Roland, who clearly hadn't taken the comment in good spirit. "I'm working on it."

Roland understood. Cotton still hadn't come around to the idea that a person could be a cannibal and not the enemy at the same time.

"I ain't gonna pretend I'm sorry," Roland said as he began walking again. "About all this. About how the world is."

"Figured as much," Cotton replied. "But what about what happened here? These were your people. You built this town."

"Remember transitory inflation?" Roland asked.

"What the hell are you talking about?"

"When things started going down the tubes and all the prices went up. They kept calling it 'transitory inflation.' I'm not an economist, but the idea was that it would be short-lived. Prices would bump up, but then they'd go back down again like a wave. Of course, that was all bullshit; Washington just didn't want to cause a panic when gas hit twenty dollars a gallon. Well, that's the way I see civilization now. It's transitory. When we started setting this place up, this is always how I knew it would end. Maybe not exactly like this, but I knew it would end."

"You think the people here knew that?"

"Probably not. Most of them, if they were being honest about it, were still hoping things would get back to normal someday, whatever the hell that means."

"Internet, movies, social media," Cotton said. "That's probably what it meant for most people."

"All bullshit. No one's life really meant anything on that treadmill. Now, even if it's short and brutal, at least your life *means* something."

"And when did you become a philosopher?"

"Ain't philosophy, friend. Just the truth." Roland stopped again and turned to Cotton. "Speaking of which, there's something I need to let you in on."

"What's that?"

Roland reached into his back pocket and retrieved Zhukov's journal. "Found this back at Marble Falls."

"I saw you take it," Cotton replied.

"And you didn't say anything?" Roland asked. "I'm starting to think you don't trust me."

"It's not like that," Cotton said. "I just know you like to win."

"Last time I read the Bible, I didn't see that listed in the 'do-not-do' category."

"Winning ain't the problem," Cotton replied. "It's what it turns people into. It's what you do to make it happen. Ends justify the means and all that."

"Either way, what's in this journal makes for some pretty interesting bedtime reading. Particularly the part about the epicenter of everything that's happened and the folks who started it."

Cotton's eyes widened. "That was the Russian's journal, wasn't it?" he asked. "The one I was fighting. The one Fred killed."

"That's right. He's some kind of apocalypse

detective the Russkies sent here. From the looks of it, they're just trying to smooth the way for their invasion force. Want to make sure no other Jacks are about to pop out of the box."

"Like black-eyed cannibals."

"Exactly." Roland visibly hesitated for a moment and then went on. "This guy, Zhukov, he also had an idea that these folks are holed up someplace and are maybe waiting to pull the trigger on something else."

"Because the black-eyed cannibals ain't enough?"

Roland smiled, on the verge of laughing.

"What?" Cotton asked.

"It's just ... we've got three Tier One guys together and not one of us has made a Black Eyed Peas joke yet."

Cotton laughed. Gallows humor was a trademark of the men in their line of work, and the obvious joke not being exploited was a clear miss.

"So, where did he think these guys are?" Cotton asked.

"His best guess was New Orleans."

Cotton grimaced. "Kind of feels like I'm going backwards."

"Sometimes you gotta go back to go forward."

Cotton looked Roland squarely in the eyes. "I think you need to talk to Fred."

"I thought you trusted me," Roland said to Fred, looking visibly disappointed.

Fred shot Cotton a dirty look. "Well, you weren't supposed to find out about that."

"I didn't give him any names," Cotton interjected. "But we're all on the same side here, and I think we need to start acting like it. Myself included."

"I didn't tell you because I didn't want you to go looking for him," Fred explained. "Greg is a very private person."

"Tell him the other part," Cotton said.

"There might be an EMP coming."

Roland raised an eyebrow. "Say what now?"

"A global-event-sized EMP," Fred went on. "The kind of thing humanity can't come back from. Or at least, that's the plan."

"And let me guess," Roland said, "we need to stop it?"

"Can't let something like that happen," Cotton said. "Not if there's something we can do about it."

"So the lights go out," Roland exclaimed. "What difference does it make?"

"I don't think the vaccine was ever supposed to work," Fred said. "I don't think the aftereffects were an accident."

"What do you mean?" April asked as she continued to work on the never-ending project that was patching up Sheila. The rest of the group had been standing by throughout the conversation.

"Because it lines up with the project I was working on. With the projections for this second event they were talking about. I believe they thought turning most of the population into cannibals would annihilate us, but it didn't. As is usually the case with humans, we adapted to it."

"So they upped the ante," Cotton said. "Turned up the volume until we couldn't adapt."

"That's about the size of it," Fred replied. "The EMP isn't just about turning out the lights; it's about removing our last chance for survival. Think about it. Think about how fast and strong the first generation black-eyed cannibals were. You saw them, Sheila, right?"

Sheila nodded. "We didn't stand a chance," she said. "They went through this town like a hot knife through butter. Those things I killed at the gate were nothing."

"Only myself, Sheila, Jorge, and Harris have gone up against them," Fred said and then pointed at Roland and Cotton. "You two haven't. April and Jean haven't. If the lights go out and we're trapped in the dark with millions of those things, we die. Plain and simple."

"Okay," Roland said. "I get it. Assuming this EMP is really coming, does this guy Greg know how to stop it?"

Fred was silent for a moment and then shrugged. "I don't know, but it's the only shot we have. If anyone out there knows how to put the brakes on this thing, it's him."

"Where is he?"

"Yeah ..." Cotton sighed. "That's the challenging part."

"He's in Houston," Fred said.

"Surrounded by a million screaming cannibals."

"Well, why didn't you say so?" Roland asked with a smile. "I've been itching for a road trip ever since this bullshit started."

Sheila turned to the entrance of the veterinary clinic turned infirmary and her face changed. She felt a slow chill rolling up her spine as she heard the murmuring in her head. It wasn't just the woman, there were others as well, and somehow Sheila knew that these other voices were inside of the woman's head. They were like echoes Sheila was able to pick up.

"She's here," Sheila said suddenly.

April stopped the bandaging job she was doing on the woman's arm and looked into her eyes. They were different. April couldn't quite explain, even to herself, the intuition she had that Sheila was no longer alone inside of her own head.

"Who?" April asked.

"After the first explosion in the armory, I lost my hearing," Sheila explained. "That was when I first heard her. I thought I was going crazy, but now I know I'm not. She's real, and she's at the front gate."

Cotton and Roland looked at each other.

"I *do not* like the sound of that," Roland said.

The eight quickly re-outfitted with ARs, ammunition, and water before beginning the trek across town to the main gate.

"We need to talk," Jorge said as he walked beside Sheila.

Sheila smiled. "Great thing about this hearing

loss," she said. "You just sound like Charlie Brown's parents talking under water."

He stepped ahead of her and turned so that she could read his lips. "We need to put a pin in this," Jorge said. "You know why I did what I did. Are you going to hold it against me forever?"

"It wasn't your choice to make," Sheila said. "Not for all of us."

"But I did it," Jorge said. "And I can't take it back, even if I wanted to."

"Which you don't."

"*Damn right!*" Jorge snapped. "That son-of-a-bitch got what he had coming, and I just happened to be the one to deliver it. But I wasn't the only one who had a score to settle, and you know it."

Sheila stopped. "What do I have to say to get through to you?" she urged. "Tell me, because I'll say it! We can't get back to where we were because you're not the man I thought you were. So, let it go!"

Jorge stared at her for a moment and then nodded. For the first time, he really understood. She was right. He had changed, not just since taking the shot that killed the President of the United States, but also over the past forty-eight hours. He was a million miles away from the man she had lain beside for so many nights.

"Okay," he said, and he turned to walk away.

"*Holy shit*," Cotton said as he walked to the front gate at the lead of the group.

"It's her," Harris said.

"And it looks like she brought a few friends," Roland added.

A few hundred feet beyond the gate stood June Kennedy. Her blood-soaked dress was matted to her skin, and her dead, black eyes stared at the group as they approached the entrance to Oatmeal. Several hundred feet behind her stood what could only be described as an ocean of black-eyed cannibals.

"How many do you think there are?" April asked.

"Enough," Jean replied simply.

"Few thousand at least," Jorge commented as he scanned the road.

"Nowhere near that number of people were vaccinated between Oatmeal, Cypress Mill, and Tow," Fred surmised. "She's *collecting* them. Drawing them in, like a magnet."

"We keep talking about the million in Houston," Cotton said. "But it's a pretty safe bet the rest of the City States all received the same vaccine. If that's true, how many do you think we're really dealing with? How many can her magnet pull in?"

"Ten million," Fred replied. "Assuming they still had the manufacturing up from the first generation of the vaccine and they rolled it out to the different City States about the same time. Could be more."

"Well, I think we need to deal with the several thousand on our doorstep first," Roland interjected. "Before we get super-concerned about the ten million."

"I'll go," Sheila said.

"Are you nuts?" Jorge snapped.

"We're connected. It's just like I said—I hear her in my head. I don't know why, but I do. She knows me. If I can somehow get her to leave or to let us go, we have a chance. You must know this is a fight you can't win, right?"

"She's right," Cotton said. "She'll roll over us like a speed bump in a quiet neighborhood. We need to find a different way out of this."

Before Cotton had finished his sentence, Sheila was already walking through the front gate.

June stood in silence and watched the woman walking toward her. She remembered her from months prior, during a supply exchange between Oatmeal and Cypress Mill. She had been accompanying the driver. June had thought Sheila seemed like a rough sort, perhaps someone who had not minded the end of the world very much. June also recalled the woman having both arms the last time she'd seen her.

The Evolved were chattering in her head, voicing their desire to overrun the town and consume these people, but June understood there was more at stake than just a quick meal. Her intuition was telling her that these people knew something, and she wanted to let that play out. As long as she was in the woman's head, June would always know where they were, so there was no need to destroy them. Not yet, at least. They were more use to her alive.

More and more, it was becoming obvious to June that the Evolved would not be much use to the world without a leader; without her at the helm. Were it not for the stewardship of June Kennedy, they most likely would have eaten each other by now. Considering this, she tapped her dress pocket where the bottle of pills still resided. She would need to refill them soon, somehow.

Sheila stopped within a dozen feet of June.

"You are a force to be reckoned with, aren't you, Sheila?" June asked with a smile.

"High praise," Sheila replied.

June cocked her head to the side. "You're not afraid, are you?"

"I'm fresh out of fear, lady," Sheila replied. "We just want a truce."

"You killed my children," June said.

"Your 'children?'" Sheila asked.

"Well, maybe 'grandchildren' is more appropriate, but, yes, you killed them. I know. I witnessed it."

"In my head," Sheila said.

June nodded. "Why do you think that is?" she asked. "Why is it you and I are linked?"

"I couldn't give a shit," Sheila replied. "Like I said, we just want to walk."

"And if I say no?" June asked. "What then?"

"I pull the knife in my boot and give you a little something we call a Texarkana Smile," Sheila said. "I figure your children over there will still tear me limb from limb, but as long as I get you first, I won't be raw about it."

June laughed out loud. "I like you, Sheila." She seemed to hesitate for a moment. "I think I'll let you and your friends go, for now. We have business up north either way. Do you know the Russians are here?"

"I might have heard something about that."

"We're going to address that problem, but then we'll be back. You know I'm in your head, and I'll find you wherever you go."

"And what happens when you find me?" Sheila ventured.

The question seemed to catch June strangely off guard. "That is perhaps something we will not understand until the time comes."

CHAPTER 11

Colonel Lebedev stood on the small hilltop and overlooked what remained of the Third Motor Rifles Division of the Russian Army. The rest of the Alpha Group unit was still out collecting what information they could and searching for survivors, but so far, none had been found.

"What could have done this?" Warrant Officer Balakin asked as he lowered his binoculars. "None of the equipment was damaged, and nothing was taken. Most of the men didn't even empty the magazines in their rifles."

Lebedev looked to his second-in-command. The man was clearly shaken. He could see it in his eyes.

"You don't want to say it," Lebedev said. "Despite the obvious evidence."

Balakin nodded. "They were overrun by cannibals."

"How many do you think?" Lebedev asked. "Our forces were three thousand men strong. How many would it take to slaughter them?"

"More than that," Balakin replied. "And the opposition force didn't leave a body behind, not of their own."

"Did you see the dents in the vehicles?" Lebedev asked.

"I did," Balakin confirmed. "Do you think they were using weapons of some kind? Perhaps clubs or hammers, like the ones at the farmhouse?"

"I certainly hope so," Lebedev said. "Because if not, they did this with their bare hands."

Lebedev turned to where the Communications Sergeant was running up the hill toward them. "What is it?" the Colonel asked.

The Communications Sergeant handed his commanding officer a sheathe of papers, which Lebedev looked over.

"Where were these?"

"At the intel tent," the Sergeant replied. "It seems they came in directly before the attack. Most likely, no one saw them."

"These are from Zhukov," Lebedev said, and he

handed the papers to his second. "Most likely a burst transmission before he was overrun."

Balakin looked them over for a moment and then turned to Lebedev. "Can this be true?"

Lebedev shrugged. "Zhukov might have been eccentric, but his track record with these types of investigations is immaculate. If I were a betting man and I was down to my last ruble, I'd bet it on him."

"What does this mean for us?"

"The nearest active division we could report to is in Amarillo, but we would be arriving with nothing."

"You have another idea?" Balakin asked with a raised eyebrow.

"Our charter is clear. We have sufficient authority to follow up on this to the extent we feel appropriate."

Balakin withdrew a map from his document case and quickly plotted the co-ordinates transmitted by General Zhukov, drawing a small circle in the center of the City State of Houston. He showed it to Colonel Lebedev.

"That's not an accident," Balakin said. "It's the exact center of the city."

"Right where I would be, if I did not want to be found."

A rifle fired in the distance and Balakin looked to

his left, toward the source of the sound. It was one of theirs. Then there was another, and another and another. He snatched his radio from his vest and keyed it.

"This is Command, report."

There was a moment of silence, just static on the radio, but in that moment both Balakin and Lebedev could see what was happening.

"Mother of God," Balakin said quietly.

As if it were part of some darkly orchestrated ballet, the dead were seemingly rising from the ground and turning on the Alpha Group soldiers who were surveying the carnage.

"They're coming back! They're coming back!" A voice finally returned from the radio.

"Move to the helicopter for immediate extraction," Lebedev said calmly.

"They can't," Balakin interjected as he surveyed the battle space. "They're cut off."

Lebedev understood. The cannibals were swarming in circles around the men, cutting off any line of retreat. Several of the soldiers were attempting to break through and assist their comrades, but it was to no avail. They were hopelessly outnumbered.

"Grab the PKP!" Lebedev shouted, indicating

the heavy machine gun secured in the helicopter. He began heading down the hill to his men.

"Stop!" Balakin ordered.

Lebedev did stop, perhaps shocked more than anything else by what sounded like an order from his subordinate.

"What did you say?"

"You cannot help them!" Balakin continued as he did indeed pull the machine gun and as much ammo as he could retrieve from the Mi-17 helicopter. He handed a heavy bag of explosives to the Comms Sergeant. "But you can continue the mission and get that information to someone who can use it."

"Are you mad?" Lebedev shouted. "We cannot just leave them to die!"

"We can and we will," Balakin countered. "They are soldiers. It's what they do."

"No," Lebedev said as he shook his head. "We will find a way."

"I have found a way," Balakin said as he unholstered his pistol and pointed it at his commander. "And if you do not get on that helicopter now you will die on this hill."

In a sudden moment of clarity, Lebedev knew that his Warrant Officer was right. He made sure that the sheathe of papers the Comms Sergeant had collected from the intelligence tent was secured in his cargo pocket and he walked to where the air transportation sat.

No words were exchanged, no final goodbyes as Balakin dropped the bipod for the PKP and quickly deployed the machine gun against the black-eyed cannibals swarming up the hill. The Comms Sergeant stood behind him hurling explosives down into the churning mass of bodies, but their cause was a hopeless one, and they knew it. Their only goal was to buy time for their commanding officer.

Lebedev secured himself into the pilot's seat and began the process of getting the rotors turning, preparing the vehicle for takeoff. He tried not to look at what was happening outside as he worked, knowing it would only distract him from the task at hand.

After what seemed like a lifetime (though it was only a few minutes) the helo lifted from the ground and Lebedev turned it ninety degrees, enough to see what was happening below. Most of the arms had been stripped from the aircraft to allow for transport of Alpha Group men and materials, and he had no way of firing the door mounted 7.62 machine gun that remained. All he could do was watch as Warrant Officer Balakin and the Comms

Sergeant made their desperate last stand on the hilltop.

Colonel Lebedev knew it was pointless to linger, and so he turned the vehicle and began his flight toward the City State of Houston. The last thing he saw was Warrant Officer Balakin hurling empty ammunition cans at the seemingly endless wave of the black-eyed beasts.

Roland led the group to Oatmeal's motor pool, and as he walked, he surveyed the scores of the dead. Some were the infected Sheila had killed, but many had been killed in the first wave of the attack by the first black-eyed Cannibals. He had pretended that it didn't bother him when Cotton had asked, acted like it was just part of the gig, but that wasn't the truth. Roland Reese did indeed feel something for the people who had been part of the community he had worked so hard to build, but he had no idea how to process those feelings.

Growing up in a broken home and then living out of a suitcase, shuffling from group home to group home, had not ingrained in him the tools he needed to build connections and to understand the profound meaning of the loss of those connections. Until the time came that he did understand those concepts, Roland would continue to wear the mask of the callous warrior that had served him well for so long.

"Jesus," April said as they turned on the lights, powered by the collections of solar panels that had been set up throughout the town.

They understood what had happened in the large garage. A group of about a dozen people from the town had tried to barricade themselves inside and make a stand against the first wave of black-eyed cannibals; the ones that were incredibly strong, fast, and aggressive. They had failed, but, importantly, they had known they were going to fail.

Eleven bodies were slumped against the wall, all of them facing it with a corresponding blood splatter on the concrete. One last body was collapsed in the middle of the floor with a pistol beside him. Knowing what was about to happen, this man had lined everyone up against the wall and taken their lives, before ending his own to avoid being devoured alive.

Jorge placed a hand on Fred's shoulder. The woman was clearly on the verge of breaking down, but the element of human touch seemed to help her calm down.

"He did the right thing," Jean said.

Cotton looked down at his daughter, back into

those cold eyes. "Can I talk to you outside?" he asked.

Cotton took a knee so that he was eye-to-eye with his daughter.

"Are you okay?" he asked.

"Couldn't be better," Jean said with a smile. "How about you?"

Cotton couldn't help but laugh at the way she'd asked the question. "Yeah, I'm hanging in there. It's just ... you're not acting like yourself."

"Maybe I wasn't acting like myself before," Jean countered. "Because maybe I didn't know who I really was."

"And now you do?"

"I always wanted this."

"Wanted what?" Cotton asked.

"War."

Her answer took Cotton aback. "What do you mean?"

"My whole life, I grew up hearing you and the boys talking about it. Telling your stories. Seeing how it changed you. I wanted that experience."

Cotton had thought about it many times—about how if he'd had a son, he would have expected the boy to want to follow in his father's footsteps—but it had never occurred to him that his only daughter might want the same thing. It should have made sense, though. The girl had essentially grown up in the SEAL Teams. She'd been around warriors her entire life, and she'd spent time on the compounds and on the ranges. She'd even studied land navigation with her father for fun.

"Guess I can't give you the same speech I used to give young men about not knowing what you're signing up for until you get there—because you've been there."

"And I'm still here," Jean added. "I know the risks now. I know what happens."

"And you know you might die."

"Ain't no 'might' about it," Jean said. "I'm already dead."

"Don't say that."

Jean smiled. "Don't you get it yet? We all are. Always were. When I was up on that hill at the rail yard, makin' it rain, I wasn't afraid. I wasn't worried about those boys coming at me because I understand that we're just living on borrowed time. Nothing wrong with that. Sooner we all understand it, easier this gets."

Part of Cotton wanted to push back, to make his

daughter understand that her words weren't true and that they could still have a bright future, but another part of him knew that she was right.

Maybe *he* was the one who needed to be set straight, not her.

The door to the motor pool opened, and Cotton walked back inside with Jean. He stopped and looked at the vehicle Roland had unveiled. He'd noticed what looked like some kind of RV covered by a giant tarp when they'd first walked in.

"What the hell is that?" Cotton asked.

"I up-armored a Winnebago," Roland said with a smile.

"It's almost like you knew something like this was going to happen," Sheila said with a knowing look.

"How could you not know?" Roland asked incredulously. "I mean ... *shit*. I wasn't gonna put out a bulletin warning everyone their days are numbered, but you'd have to seriously have your head in the sand to not know some version of this would happen soon enough."

"Aren't you just a little ray of sunshine?" April said.

"Try not to get a sunburn, honey," Roland said with a wink.

"What about me is sexy right now?" April asked.

At this point, the woman looked as if she had been through multiple championship MMA fights and her leg was in a boot.

Cotton examined the RV and shook his head.

"What?" Roland asked. He knew a critique was coming.

"That's gotta go," Cotton said, pointing to the mounted fifty cal on the roof.

"That's the only thing I want to *stay*," Roland insisted.

"It makes us a target. Random RV driving through Texas might not attract much attention, but a random RV that looks like something out of *Mad Max* is going to look like something some group of marauders might want to take."

"Fine," Roland said. He knew Cotton was right. "Any other complaints?"

'Yeah," Cotton said. "I know you all had Polish for lunch, but Jean and I need some human food."

"I ain't cross, you know," Roland said to Fred as Cotton and Jean scrounged what little there was in the food storage. "About you keeping things from me, I mean."

"Maybe I should have trusted you more," Fred admitted. "It's just ... Look, we're not people who would probably have spent a lot of time together before, you know? Don't take that personally; it's just the truth."

"I get it," Roland said with a nod. "And I also get that I'm not an easy person to know. And to trust someone, you have to know them."

"Maybe that needs to change?"

"I ain't a man accustomed to change, if you know what I mean."

"Maybe that needs to change, too," Fred said with a smile. "Maybe that's what this new world is about. Maybe that's the blessing in disguise. We all get a chance to be someone else; to be the person we thought we were going to be a long time ago."

"Maybe."

"What do you think that looks like for you? If you don't mind me asking?"

Roland looked across the warehouse to where April was sitting with Cotton and Jean. "I don't know. Maybe the kind of guy that settles down. Someday."

"I thought you were born for war?" Fred asked, only half-joking.

"Maybe I was," Roland replied. "But after you're born, you still have to grow up."

"That's strangely profound," Fred said. "Mind a piece of advice?"

Roland studied her for a moment and then shrugged.

"I think the 'cool guy' schtick is your armor. If you really like her, in a meaningful way, just try being yourself. Maybe she'll like that guy."

"I think war is probably easier," Roland replied.

"Okay," Roland said. "This is the plan. At least, as near as I can figure. I don't rightly know if we can make things any better, but we can sure as hell try to keep them from getting a lot worse.

"We don't know how long the Cannibal Queen is going to be gone, but we can't stay here. We know that. It might be that the best use of our time is to head to Houston and see if we can locate this Dr. Wilson. From what Fred says, he may know how to keep the lights from going out. If we get really lucky, he might also know something about the Gen 2 vaccine, maybe something we can use."

"How do we get in?" Jorge asked. "That place has gotta be overrun, and even if the original Gen 2 recipients aren't there, it looks like the ones they infect turn into those half-assed versions. And I'm sure as hell there's *plenty* of them wanderin' around."

"It really depends on how many doses of the vaccine were dispensed in the first twenty-four hours," Fred said. "And whether that Cannibal Queen woman pulled all of the originals to her, or if, for some reason, they stayed."

"So, it's going to be a mess either way," April interjected.

"Gotta be done," Cotton said. "The Russians are up north, and the Chinese are almost certainly to the west and maybe even down south. East is Cannibal Town, but at least there, we have a chance."

"I think she's heading north," Sheila said.

"Why's that?" Cotton asked.

"Something she said. She made a comment about knowing the Russians are here. She said she had business with them."

"Makes sense," Cotton said. "The Russian Army is the largest food source around. Particularly if she's planning on drawing a million or more soldiers to her. They all have to be fed."

"So, we have time," Roland said. "Let's not waste it."

Cotton Wiley stood out in the cool of the evening and watched the sun setting. He warmed his hands and gave himself a moment to just breathe. The door to the motor pool opened behind him, and April walked out. Cotton looked down at her leg.

"All fixed up?" he asked.

"As much as can be expected," April replied. She pulled a cigarette from her pocket and lit it in the semi-darkness.

"Didn't know you smoked," Cotton commented.

"Never too late to start," April replied with a smile. "Quit them after college, but the apocalypse has a way of kickstarting bad habits."

"Tell me about it," Cotton replied. "Look, I've been meaning to say something about what happened the other day."

"Nothing to say," April said. "It was just a moment. As far as we knew, we were the only two folks around worth ... well, you know."

Cotton smiled. "Just so you know, I don't go

around kissing every cannibal I see."

"That's not what I hear."

Cotton laughed. "It's just ... I think Roland has a thing for you."

"I picked up on that," April said. "Didn't seem like you trusted him much this morning."

"A lot's changed since then. *I've* changed."

"Fair enough," April said with a nod. "Maybe after we stop the end of the world, I'll update my Tinder profile and see what happens."

Cotton laughed again and reached into his pocket. He pulled out the ziplock bag containing the Freedom Corridor map and extracted the folded piece of paper.

"What's that?" April asked.

"Man in the road gave it to me," Cotton replied. "It's a map to Alaska. Supposedly a way to get there without getting killed."

"Seems like that's what you've been looking for," April said.

"Lighter?" Cotton asked and held out his hand.

April handed him the lighter and watched as he activated it and then set the flame to the map. Cotton watched it burn in the darkness and then dropped it to the ground.

"Can't run no more," he said decisively.

EPILOGUE

Houston, Texas

"I want you to start working again," Doctor Gregory Wilson said as he stood in the second sub-basement of the Fulbright Tower.

The current object of his attention was one of the massive generators that had been powering the building over the past several months, since the catastrophic failure of the Texas power grid. In reality, the generators had never been intended to run the building around the clock on a permanent basis, and yet they had been doing just that, and to a capacity far beyond expectations. At least, to a point.

Over the past thirty days, the generators had

begun failing one by one. The staff of the building had been able to slow the progressive failure down, but since they had all either been turned into insane black-eyed cannibals or been devoured by the aforementioned a few days prior, that progressive failure had rapidly accelerated to the point where only one generator now remained.

And it had stopped working just minutes earlier.

Since the previously busy building at the center of Houston was now deserted, the loss of most of the generator system was not a big deal, but having zero generators would cause quite a number of associated problems. Not the least among these was keeping the building warm when the weather began turning cold, assuming it would.

The weather itself was just one more thing in this new world that had become increasingly unpredictable. Gregory wasn't certain if this was just bad timing in terms of the deterioration of the climate or if it was a man-made problem. He knew that the Chinese, specifically, had been working quite successfully on multiple projects to affect the weather, initially under the guise of wanting to improve rainfall patterns for farming. Of course, anyone in the know would understand their claims were a bunch of bull.

They wanted the technology available as a weapon.

So, it was not far outside the realm of possibilities that Beijing would choose this as the perfect time to deploy such a weapons system against the United States. It would certainly account for the super-hurricane that had struck Houston the month prior—far outside of hurricane season—and had partially flooded the entire city and blown out nearly every window in Fulbright Tower.

The flashlight in Doctor Gregory Wilson's hand flickered and he sighed. One more problem. It flickered again and then dimmed. He turned it off with the click of a button and stood in the darkness for a moment. In the insulated concrete of the sub-basement, he couldn't hear anything from the outside world. It was quiet. Peaceful.

He reached into his pocket, retrieved the smaller backup flashlight he carried, and turned it on. He turned his head to the right and stumbled backward.

The black-eyed cannibal standing in the corner of the large room was staring at him with its undying gaze.

It had to have been there the whole time. It had just been standing there, watching him. Why hadn't it done anything? Why hadn't it attacked? All of the others did, the very moment they saw fresh meat, but this one hadn't.

Then Gregory understood. The floor around it was slick with blood, and he saw the viscous fluid running down the creature's arms. It had been seriously injured and was most likely at death's door. Gregory decided to take a chance, and he moved his light to better illuminate the thing.

It was a man; a man who looked to be in his late fifties, wearing one of the jumpsuits worn by the utility workers who'd serviced the building before the apocalypse.

As Gregory studied him, he saw that the man was not quite as terrifying as he'd always thought these black-eyed cannibals were. They were generally moving so fast that it was hard to see them clearly, and when they were chasing you, it wasn't the best time to conduct an examination of them.

Gregory guessed this man was not one of the original vaccination recipients; he was one of the later infections. The reality was, he just looked like a normal man, but with black eyes and washed-out skin. Was it worth taking his investigation a step further?

"Can you ... Can you talk?" Gregory asked. "Are you able to?"

The cannibal continued to stare blankly for a moment and then opened his mouth. Blood slowly poured out, and he coughed. Gregory quickly stepped back. They knew that the original recipients of the Gen 2 vaccine were able to infect others and those infected became these weakened versions of the black-eyed cannibals, but the jury was still out on whether those copies could then infect other people as well.

Gregory decided it was probably best not to find out the hard way, and he walked quickly back to the main door. But was he really going to just lock it in the sub-basement? He knew he ought to do something to avoid a nasty surprise later, but after what felt like a lifetime in the apocalypse, he knew he still didn't have the capacity within him to kill. Even if it was one of these black-eyed creatures. Even if it was to save his own life.

The door clicked shut, and Gregory worked his key in the lock. No doubt the thing would expire on its own. Clearly the only reason it had not attacked was because it was weakened from blood loss.

Gregory returned to the stairwell and began the long trek back up to the fifty-second floor of the tower. Each door that led from the stairwell to a working floor was normally locked by the security system, and the default protocol during loss of power was for the doors to remain locked. This was important because Gregory knew that he was not alone in the building. There were at least several dozen of the black-eyed cannibals in here with him, but they were all trapped on the floor they had been on when the lockdown kicked in. He knew they would eventually starve. It was just a matter of time.

At the entrance to the fifty-first floor, he stopped and looked at the locked door. There was no reason to think they wouldn't still be in there, unless they had gone out the window and plunged to their deaths, as he'd noticed a few already had. The evidence was clear from the bodies on the concrete below. However, it had only happened a couple of times. None of the others had done it, which made Gregory think they had somehow learned from the event. They'd learned not to try it.

He still wasn't clear on how the creatures' brains worked, either the originals or the secondary infections. Each one seemed to face a unique disadvantage. Specifically, the originals were enraged and seemed to be running on much higher levels of adrenaline than a normal person—or cannibal. As a result, their judgment was clouded, and it caused them to do foolish things such as jump out of windows when they couldn't find another exit.

As for the secondaries, they had another problem entirely. They seemed almost impaired, as if they'd had one too many beers or perhaps part of their brain was turned off. This, of course, did not mean they weren't still dangerous. After the first wave of Gen 2 vaccine recipients had begun turning and then the subsequent infections had occurred, Gregory had watched enough of the slaughter in the streets below to know that both of these cannibal breeds were dangerous.

There was a thought: Cannibal *breeds*. Perhaps he could even think of them as 'variants,' which of course begged the question: Would there be other variants? So far, they were up to three different variants. White-eyed cannibals such as himself—those who had originally taken the vaccine in the hopes of escaping the virus—were, for the most part, normal people. They just happened to need human flesh to survive. These new variants, though, were taking the evolution of the human race in a potentially disturbing direction.

Gregory reached out to the door that opened onto the fifty-first floor. He hesitated for a moment and then lightly tapped it with a single finger. He was greeted by a heavy slam on the door and then a repeated banging of fists and a deep growling.

Yes, they were indeed still in there.

Gregory worked his key in the lock, and once the tumblers finally clicked into place, he pushed the door to the fifty-second floor open and breathed a sigh of relief. The floor was well lit by the solar lanterns he had dispersed around the converted living space. Even if he hadn't been able to get the generator running again, he still had his own backups that would at least make quarantine liveable.

He had already used all of the garbage bags he could find to seal up the windows as best he could, and for the moment, at least it wasn't too cold in the building. Even so, Gregory knew that the time was coming when he would have to relocate, if for no other reason than he would eventually run out of food.

Gregory walked to one of the few windows that had survived the hurricane and looked down to the streets below. They were still quite flooded, but the waters were shallow enough that the black-eyed cannibals could still walk through them. There were at least a hundred milling about on McKinney

Street. He wondered if they knew he was there, if perhaps some sort of extra-sensory perception told them there was still fresh meat about.

He also wondered why they didn't eat each other, but only preyed upon Gen 1 cannibals and (he assumed) humans.

He assumed there were still survivors like him left in the city, but they were probably also in hiding.

Gregory walked across the room to where his laptop sat on the lectern he used as his de facto workstation. He'd favored a standing desk back when he was a student earning the first of his four PhDs, and the practice had remained with him ever since. Even back then, he had intuitively known that sitting all day would eventually lead to health problems.

The Jackery solar generator sitting beside the window had so far done an excellent job of powering the devices he needed to continue his work. It also powered the small black and white television that he'd connected to the old VHS player. Yes, it was the twenty-first century and there were any number of ways he could have stored his complete collection of *The Office* in digital format, but something about the old technology spoke to him.

Gregory pulled open the laptop and waited for the screen to activate, then he opened the video conferencing application he had been using to stay connected to New Orleans over the past year.

After a moment, the messaging icon displayed a caller in the 'waiting room,' and Gregory hit the button to accept the caller. The screen flickered, and a man appeared. He was in his early sixties, with well groomed hair, and he wore a tailored suit. His eyes were white, like Gregory's, indicating that he, too, was a recipient of the Gen 1 vaccine.

The man smiled. "Good to see you, Gregory."

"You, too, Mister Rampart."

Bill Rampart was the CEO of Fluid Dynamics and had stayed connected with Doctor Gregory Wilson over the past year as the lead on the project they had dubbed 'Permanent Midnight.' Gregory privately wondered if Mister Rampart had actually seen the movie or if it was just a coincidence.

"How's your work going?" Bill Rampart asked.

"Well," Gregory replied, "I've figured out how to bounce the signal across the satellites."

"So soon?" Bill asked, the surprise on his face obvious. "I thought that would take more time."

"It really wasn't hard," Gregory replied. "It's kind of the difference between calling someone down the street or calling someone in France. If you know the number and you account for the new atmospherics we're dealing with, it's fairly simple."

"Can you transmit that code back to our analysts?" Bill Rampart asked.

"I ... can," Gregory replied slowly.

"I sense some hesitancy."

"It's just ... Are we really going to do it? Turn out the lights for the entire world?"

Bill Rampart smiled. "It's a contingency, Gregory. Like mutually assured destruction. You remember that, right? Everyone had nukes, but no one was going to use them because then everyone would lose?"

"I do."

"The concept's the same. The Russians are here. The Chinese are here. We need a weapon that will force them to leave without undue bloodshed. What you are doing will save lives. *Millions* of lives."

"And the Gen 3 vaccine?" Gregory asked.

Bill Rampart audibly sighed. "I want to tell you that it's ready to go, but it's not. We're close, but we still need more testing."

"I suppose that's good," Gregory said with a nod. "Considering what happened with the Gen 2."

He looked back to the streets below and the hordes of the black-eyed things swarming below.

"No one could have foreseen that," Bill said. "That's why we're being so fastidious with our testing this time."

"I understand."

"So, you'll transmit the code?"

"Of course," Gregory replied. "But after I do, you'll send the helicopter for me? I can't stay here, not for much longer. The generators have finally quit."

"Understood," Bill said. "Get the code packaged up and transmitted through the satellite uplink, and we'll deploy a security team to extract you."

Gregory smiled. "Will do."

"Excellent," Bill Rampart said with a smile. "And Gregory, I'm truly sorry that you have had to weather the storm there, both literally and figuratively, but what you're doing is of vital importance."

"I understand."

Bill Rampart nodded. "I assume you're still safe there? Our friends are still confined to the other floors?"

"For the moment," Gregory confirmed.

"Good to know."

. . .

Bill Rampart closed the video messaging window and slid back in his chair. He let out a breath. He was indeed too old for this much intrigue.

"Let me know when the code comes through," he said.

"Are we going to get him?" Ralph Finley, Rampart's head of security, asked.

Bill turned to the man and cocked his head to the side. "After a fashion. I want you to send two helos to the Fulbright building."

"Search and Rescue?" Ralph asked.

"No, Ralph. First, I want you to send a command to the emergency generator in the Fulbright building, the one our friend doesn't know about, to override the access locks."

Ralph nodded his understanding. "To open them."

"Yes. Once Doctor Wilson transmits his code, we will open the floodgates, so to speak. Then you will personally escort two assault teams to his location."

"Is that totally necessary?" Ralph asked. "Our estimate says there are at least a hundred of those black-eyed cannibals occupying that building."

"I learned a long time ago," Bill Rampart said, "to never leave anything to chance." He pointed to the long scar running down the side of his face. "A CIA operative named Jack Bonafide taught me that lesson the hard way, and it was one I never forgot."

"Understood," Ralph said. "It's just that I don't want to needlessly risk the lives of my men."

"Of course. But we need to keep the circle tight on this, and Doctor Wilson has a history of being very fickle as to whose side he's on. With the Russians and the Chinese on our doorstep, we cannot afford to leave him with the chance of handing this code over to them."

"In that case, I'll get to work," Ralph said and headed for the door, then he stopped and turned back to his employer. "Do you mind if I ask you something?"

"Ask away."

"I know you've heard the rumors about the black-eyed cannibals."

"I have," Bill Rampart said with a knowing smile.

"It's just that ... we haven't actually gone up against them before. If we're going to fly right into the center of the hornet's nest and go head-to-head with them, I need every piece of intel I can get."

"Understood."

"So ... is it true?" Ralph asked with some obvious hesitancy.

"That we created them on purpose? That the vaccine was designed to fail?"

"Yes."

"Of course not," Bill Rampart replied with a smile and a shake of his head. "I'm not insane."

***

"I don't know, I don't know, I don't know," Doctor Gregory Wilson repeated quietly as his finger hovered over the button that would transmit his code to Fluid Dynamics in New Orleans.

It wasn't that he didn't trust Mister Rampart. He believed they needed a so-called 'nuclear option' to stop the invading Russian and Chinese armies. He also understood that the invasion was not even the worst-case scenario. The worst possible outcome was that those two armies would eventually use America as their final battleground, to decide who would quite possibly conquer the world.

It was madness to think that the best-case scenario here was to send the entire planet back to the Stone Age, but that was exactly what would happen. His code would seize every satellite orbiting the earth, daisy-chain them together, and then send an electromagnetic pulse strong enough to fry every electronic device on earth, even the ones that were supposedly safe. In fact, it could quite possibly start some fires, but there was no way around that. It was just the nature of the beast he had designed.

Gregory's finger hovered for another moment and then finally dropped on the key.

Click.

Sent.

"Well, no going back now," he said to himself as he walked to the window.

The darkness of the city stretched out before him, but he took comfort in the fact that, soon enough, the helicopters would be coming for him. Flight time from New Orleans to Houston couldn't be very much. He might even find himself in a warm bed within a matter of hours.

Gregory narrowed his eyes and leaned forward.

"What is that?" he asked himself as he watched a single green flare sail up from the ground.

It looked as if it had been sent up from the edge of the city, but it couldn't be Mister Rampart's team. It was far too soon, and they would be landing on the helicopter pad atop the building, not on the outskirts of the city.

Then the lights came on.

"What the hell?" Gregory asked as he turned to look at the overhead lights.

"*Manual override engaged,*" a pre-recorded female voice said as the heavy *clank* of doors unlocking reverberated throughout the building. "*Doors unlocked.*"

Doctor Gregory Wilson looked around the now dimly lit top floor and then back to his own reflection in the window.

"Oh dear."

**The story continues in…
Book Three: The Dead And The Wasted
on Amazon!**

If you enjoyed this book please consider providing a review on Amazon.

ABOUT THE AUTHOR

Jordan Vezina is a fiction writer living in Austin, Texas with his wife Emily where they run a business together. Jordan served in both the Marine Corps and Army Infantry, and worked as a bodyguard. This background provided much of the detail regarding weapons and tactics in Jordan's books.

jordanvezina.com
hello@jordanvezina.com

Printed in Great Britain
by Amazon